One Last Night

Fated Lovers – Book 2

SOTIA LAZU

Cover Artist: Erin Dameron-Hill
Editor: Graham R. Rooles
ISBN: 978-0692623671

Manufactured in the United States of America
Acelette Press

"If it's true love, it's fated." ~X.

Table of Contents

Chapter One

"So you're a chef?" She was close, her lips almost touching his ear. Still, he barely made out her words. It wasn't just the music blasting from the speakers next to them, it was the way his body hummed at her closeness. He'd never responded to anyone the way he did to her presence.

Mike ran his fingers down her spine, enjoying the silky material of her dress almost as much as he enjoyed her pale blonde hair tickling his neck. "Yes. I'm actually a silent partner in *Arbore's*," he said. That line was usually a closer, now the Italian restaurant he worked for was up and happening again.

"No, actually. You're not," she said with a little laugh. "I still can't believe Derek let you get away with this for so long."

Her laugh, throaty and full, had sent an electric jolt through Mike, but her words made him stop caressing her back. "You know Derek?" Was she Derek's family? Nah,

Mike would have met her before. Maybe she was related to Amanda?

The blonde pulled his ear lobe between her lips, and worried it with her teeth. "Do you wanna talk about this some more, or do you wanna fuck me?"

"Where?" Figuring things out could wait.

"Ladies' room."

He nodded. "You go first, and I'll be there in two."

"Or we could both go now." She licked a trail up the side of his neck. Bit him lightly.

She was either the coolest or the craziest chick ever. He didn't care to figure out which, because she was definitely the hottest, and that was all that mattered. He stood and held out his hand. She grabbed it, jumped up, and let him lead her downstairs.

The lack of a queue was a miracle, but Mike wouldn't have minded cutting in front of an army, to get inside the blonde next to him as soon as possible.

"I don't even know your name," he whispered in her ear. He didn't have to duck his head; in her high heels, she stood almost as tall as he did. Which would work out awesomely for standing-up sex. For any kind of sex, really. The woman was a goddess.

She seemed to consider it a moment. "Ana," she said. "Call me Ana."

"But it's not your real name?" That was a lame-ass question to ask. Especially after he'd lied about what he did for a living—well, the chef part was true. Mostly.

"It's a nickname I haven't used in a while," she said.

Sudden panic ripped through his lust-addled brain. "Wait. Are you legal?" She looked mid-twenties, but he couldn't risk it.

"Twenty-six last week. Want to card me?"

He might have, but she pushed him against the tiled wall and shoved her tongue in his mouth before the door swung closed behind them.

At a loss for words or not, he wasn't the type to sit back and watch, while a gorgeous, horny woman had her way with him. He held her and spun, so she was sandwiched between him and the door. "I've wanted you since you walked in the restaurant," he said. He wedged one thigh between her legs and busied his fingers with undoing his belt.

She nibbled on his jaw. "I know. It's why I asked you for a drink." She angled her hips, and naked wet flesh slid against his knuckles.

"Fuck."

"I knew you'd appreciate it."

Had she taken her panties off at some point between the restaurant and the club? She'd certainly had time to; she'd had dinner before nine, but waited for him to get off his shift at one in the morning. Irrational jealousy flooded his veins at the thought that maybe she'd left her home without underwear, hoping to meet someone—anyone—to give her a dirty fuck.

"Was it for me?" He managed an easy, conversational tone, as he slipped a finger inside her. She was hot and tight, and he could barely hold back from shoving his cock inside her to the hilt.

Her gasp turned into a mewl, as he withdrew his hand and rubbed the blunt head of his cock against her clit. "Always for you," she said.

Since she'd never laid eyes on him before tonight, her answer was a blatant lie, but it was good for his ego nonetheless. "Want my dick?" he asked.

"Yes." She met and held his gaze, and there was a challenge in those baby-blue eyes that he couldn't ignore.

He took a step back and fished a condom out of his back pocket. Letting her stand there and watch him, he tore the packaging with his teeth, and took his time rolling the latex down his length. She liked watching. He could tell. "Beg me for it," he said, closing the distance between them.

"*Please.*"

He slanted his mouth to hers and took his time tasting her lips. He needed to do this his way, needed to regain control of the situation, before he lost it like a horny teenager. When he felt her melt against him, her tongue seeking his, he whispered, "Turn around."

She did, and he bent her over the nearest sink.

"Please fuck me. Now, Mike." Their gazes met in the mirror, and hers held longing the likes of which he'd never seen before.

Bullshit. She was just up for a good time. And wasn't that a lucky coincidence?

He skimmed his palms up the back of her thighs, lifting the hem of her dress and tracing the perfect curve of her ass. Then, one hand on her lower back, he began easing his length inside her, not taking his eyes off her reflection.

Her eyes were half closed, her face tense with anticipation. Her full lips formed a perfect *oh*. He regretted turning her away from him. He wanted to kiss those lips. "You're so fucking beautiful."

"No," she said.

Mike froze in place. Had she changed her mind? Had he done something wrong? "Should I stop?"

"*God*, no." She twisted her body, fisted one hand in his shoulder-length hair, and pulled him to her for a ferocious kiss that left his lips feeling swollen. "Stop being gentle. I want you to fuck me. Give me all you've got. And no talking."

Mike had never been one to look a gift horse in the mouth. He pushed inside her, and began thrusting as hard and fast as his need for release commanded. He could see her knuckles whiten with the intensity of her hold on the porcelain, and he dug his fingers in her hips and moved even harder, until the sink began rattling.

When she tried to pull away, he held her in place by the nape of her neck and smacked her ass with enough force to leave a red hand print. "Tell me if you want me to stop," he whispered, caressing the flushed skin.

"I will."

Ana pushed back, and he snaked a hand around her to rub her clit at the rhythm of his thrusts.

She threw her head back, and Mike draped his body over hers and swept her blonde mane out of the way so he could lick the salty sweat trickling down her neck.

Everything about the woman was perfect, from her throaty moans, to the way she clenched around him. He could hear people outside. Their coupling was no longer a secret, but all he cared about was the heavenly pussy he was pounding. He took in her blissful look, eyes hooded with desire, but gaze never wavering from his as he drove their pleasure to ever higher peaks. She was the most erotic creature he'd ever met.

And when she came… The way she gave in to it, her body thrashing beneath him, her perfect teeth digging into the full flesh of her lower lip — if Mike believed in dating, he might have asked her out right then.

As things stood, he let her ride out her orgasm, before focusing on expediting his. In mere seconds, he was almost there, but Ana's voice cut through his lust-induced haze.

"Wait. Want you in my mouth."

He pulled out, snapped off the rubber, and watched her sink to her knees in front of him. He hadn't allowed her much space to negotiate her new position, but she managed to fold her long, lithe body, and wrap her luscious lips around the head of his cock.

He was already coming, when she took him down her throat, and she kept swallowing until he was spent.

If he weren't the shallowest man on earth, he might have fallen for her right there and then.

Ana licked his cock clean and arched an eyebrow. "Are you going to help me up?"

"Of course." He was pretty sure he stammered. He pulled her up and to him, and gave her a lingering kiss — hey, if she was okay with swallowing his come, least he could do was taste it.

"Can I have your number?" he asked before he could stop himself.

She shook her head and gave him that same little laugh that said she knew so much more than he thought she did. "Oh, Mike, we both know you aren't the guy to call back. I'd better go first this time." She smoothed down her dress and raked her fingers through her hair. "Do I look like I was just fucked?"

"Very."

"Oh, well." She threw the door open and walked out, before he had time to tuck himself in.

Chapter Two

Bella reached for the alarm clock without lifting her face from her pillow. She miscalculated, and instead of hitting the snooze button, ended up tossing the stupid thing on the hardwood floor. She heard it roll under the bed. That was what she got for wanting a designer alarm clock. If it were less curvy and stylish, it might stay put once in a while.

Shit. Now she had to get up if she wanted the demonic ringing to ever stop. At least she got to finish her dream before she woke up.

She rolled to her back and stretched, feeling pleasantly sore. Inexplicably sore. She remembered his hands on her. The rough palms. The long fingers. She hadn't seen much of him naked, but the black T-shirt fit him like a second skin, stretching across the expanse of his chest and straining over his back and shoulders, defining muscle she wanted to have licked.

She'd tasted some of him, all right.

She ran her palm over her face and shook off the memories. They served no purpose other than to add to the melancholy that was today.

Could she possibly stay in bed?

The alarm clock ruled out that option.

Bella dragged her ass to the edge of the bed and let her legs fall over the side. "Will you please shut up, already?" She ducked and closed her fingers around the mostly plastic cylinder. "I should have gotten a voice-responsive model, damn it." Maybe she would this afternoon, as a treat for going through all that and coming out stronger.

And only a little bit lonely.

She huffed and clapped her hands once. "Water. Room temp," she said. "And start coffee maker." A shower and an iced coffee should help lift her spirits.

At least she thought so, until her gaze fell on her wedding ring, discarded by the side of the sink. Where it had been, for over three months now. The sight never failed to cause fresh pain, but she refused to do something about it. She needed the reminder of the hurt he'd caused, so she wouldn't slip and take his call next time.

She ran the perfect, room-temperature water and splashed some on her face, before studying her reflection in the mirror. Her eyes looked tired, because they were tired. Tired of crying over a cheater, who didn't have the balls to admit his guilt when he was caught in the act.

She might have been more lenient, if she hadn't given up everything for him. She might have forced herself to give him another chance if there were children keeping them together, but all they had was their unconditional love for each other. And he'd betrayed her and left her with nothing. He ripped her life and her heart in two, and he compounded his offense by lying about it, even after she showed him the pictures.

After fourteen years of marriage—sixteen years with him—the lie hurt maybe more than the fact he'd put his cock inside a stranger.

Bella felt faint and grasped the sink. Cold and solid, it anchored her. It also brought to mind memories of the previous night. Of another night, so many years ago.

Things had been different then, of course. She'd been easy prey for the experienced man, who seduced her with his sure touch and deep voice. She'd enjoyed every minute of that seduction, as much as she enjoyed taking the lead last night.

"Last night never happened," she told her image.

Her navy-blue pantsuit waited for her, hung outside her closet. It was crisply ironed and smelled of freshness. She almost regretted having to wear it on the drive to her lawyer's office.

A text flashed on the screen of her cell phone when she was at the door.

Please reconsider. Hear me out before you sign. This has to be a mistake.

There'd been a mistake all right, when he slipped and fell into another woman's cunt. Bella wanted to reconsider. She wanted to forget the whole thing. She wanted to believe him. Sometimes she caught herself right before calling him. Her existence had revolved around him for so long, and now she'd lost her center.

Because he went and got lost between another woman's thighs, the fucker.

Bella needed to destroy something. Obliterate it, like he obliterated their years together. She picked up the ugly-ass statue her cousin Angie had given her, and hefted it in her hand. It would have made a nice dent in the cheater's head, and would no doubt crumble to pieces against a wall, but she didn't want to waste the gift. She snorted. The ceramic miniature depicted the Aztec god Xochipilli, also known as the Prince of Flowers, and it was supposed to be a good-luck charm. It hadn't exactly worked, but Angie loved it, and Bella wouldn't trash it.

Instead, she grabbed the crystal swan that sat on the coffee table, and smashed it into the fireplace, enjoying both the brilliant sound and the million shards that reflected the morning light.

Her glee didn't last long, once she remembered she'd given the cleaning lady the week off. Eh, she'd deal with that later. First she had to go sign the official dissolution of her marriage.

San Francisco hadn't changed much the past decade and a half, but the air had gotten cleaner. Bella didn't miss the smell of car exhaust, though she did miss the rumbling purr of her old car. This one was completely quiet and allowed her to hear her thoughts all too well. And her thoughts returned to last night much more often that she was comfortable with.

The throbbing between her legs brought to mind the way he'd thrust inside her, unable to control his passion. She rubbed against the inseam of her pants and felt a deep ache. Had she masturbated in her sleep? It'd make sense, with the tricks her subconscious was playing on her.

She still couldn't believe how vivid the images and sensations had been. Incredible what her subconscious had dredged up from the deep freezer that held her happy memories. She'd been so young in her dream, but filled with the self-assurance she'd felt in her late thirties — before he turned her in an insecure mess.

She wouldn't think of him. She'd think of the young chef, who lied to get laid and looked at her like she was the most beautiful woman on earth. She barked a laugh. She really needed to get out there and get some, in real life.

She left the car in an underground parking lot, keycard in the slot, and scanned her phone at the entrance hub. "Two hours, max," she said to the microphone.

A heartbeat later, she heard the beep that signified a successful transaction. "Thank you," she told the empty space and crossed the pavement to the nearest elevator. The doors slid open the moment she pressed the button. At least something was going her way.

Or not.

She was checking her email as she entered the cabin, and didn't look up until she heard a voice call her name.

"Ana?" It was barely more than a whisper, but it hit her like a punch to the stomach. "You cut your hair."

She tugged at the short strand that barely reached her chin. She'd cut it to spite him; he always loved her long blonde tresses.

"Ana, please listen to me. I don't know who sent you these pictures and why, but I never cheated on you."

She refused to raise her gaze toward him.

"Please, baby. You have to believe me." He approached her with slow, tentative steps, as if she were a wounded animal — and wasn't she?

Why wouldn't the stupid elevator move faster? She couldn't breathe when he was so close. She couldn't be strong, when all she could think of was how she'd die for one more night in his arms.

He stood in front of her now. She could see his shoes. Black, patent, and shiny. Shiny like the pictures in her email, that showed him with that redhead. Looked barely twenty. Younger than Bella was when they started dating.

The elevator stopped, but the doors took an eternity to open.

He reached for her hand. "You know there's been nobody but you. Since the night we met, I didn't even think of another woman. Ever."

She looked up and gulped. He was painfully beautiful. His hair was shorter than back then, showing his graying temples, and his dark-brown eyes were filled with infinite pain, but he was as striking as the first time their gazes met across a crowded restaurant. His body was well defined under his button-down—who ironed that for him?—and the lines framing his mouth were as sexy as ever.

And he would still play her for a fool, if she let him.

A shy smile began curving his lips, and she realized he'd mistaken her silence for consent to keep trying. To keep lying to her.

"I'm signing the papers," she said, her voice low but heavy with finality. This time, she'd be the one making the hard choices. "We're done, Mike. For good."

Chapter Three

He was on his shift, thinking of Ana.

This was all manners of fucked up.

Her name wasn't even Ana, for all he knew.

Not that he cared. He didn't want to get to know the woman. He only wished he'd spent some more time with her heavenly body. He imagined her riding him, her golden hair whipping from side to side, as she gave into the pleasure overtaking her.

He imagined gliding his palm over her stomach. Between her breasts. Around them. Cupping them and bringing each nipple to his mouth, to lavish with attention.

He was stroking the fucking tomatoes, for fuck's sake.

"You good?"

Mike looked up from the chopping board he was putting to no use, to see Derek watching him from across the kitchen pass. "I'm fine," he said. "Banging out. We could use an extra pair of hands, boss."

"You can't pay me enough to come closer, after how you were molesting those tomatoes." Derek chuckled. "Had fun last night?"

"Fuckin' A."

"Seeing her again?"

"Nope."

"Figured. Now, haul ass. We'll be at capacity tonight."

"When aren't we?" Mike grinned, scanning the dining area. The place had blossomed after Derek got it back from his hateful ex. They couldn't accommodate walk-ins any longer—a feat, since *Arbore's-San Francisco* had been a dive a couple months back.

"I'm not complaining about it." Derek gave him a toothy grin.

His boss had nothing to complain about lately. It was weird seeing him so utterly happy since he and Amanda got together.

Some men just needed the right woman in their lives.

Mike shook his head and began dicing the tomatoes. He wasn't one of those men. The right woman for him changed every night, and he didn't mind that one bit. Maybe tonight it'd be the brunette by the entrance, who seemed not to enjoy the company of the elderly couple dining with her.

Pale blonde hair framing a heart-shaped face came to mind. Baby-blue eyes looking at him with knowledge beyond her years. *Ana.* He wouldn't mind seeing more of her. One more time, to take his time tasting —

"Shit. I know that look. You're daydreaming. She must have been special." Derek was still there. Awesome.

The usual clanging-and-yelling background noise ceased. Mike couldn't believe everyone stopped what they were doing, to eavesdrop on the two of them. "What are you all looking at? Back to work. We have mouths to feed."

Ana had a heavenly mouth. Her lips looked and felt gorgeous, stretched around his cock. He never saw her nipples, but he pictured them a pale, rosy pink. He pictured her glistening pussy to be a lighter shade. Why didn't he go down on her? Now he'd never know how she quivered when his tongue flicked her clit.

He scooped the tomatoes into the hot pan and crushed a clove of garlic with the flat of his blade. He needed to scrub his thoughts clean of Ana, and he could think of no better way than by pouring his focus into chopping, slicing, and dicing.

The real chef of *Arbore's* would never dream of doing his own prep, but the real chef of *Arbore's* was hospitalized three days ago, along with his sous-chef. Car crash, not food poisoning.

Derek was looking to replace them for however long it took their limbs to mend, but Mike already had the skills, so he took over until they found someone else. Right now, the restaurant needed a chef more than it needed a manager.

Mike watched the tomatoes shimmer, lose their water, and become nice and sticky with released sugars, before he added fresh olive oil. Garlic, in. Salt and pepper, in. Mike's mom taught him this pasta sauce, and it would never be deemed posh enough for the re-launched restaurant, so it wasn't on the menu. Table 23 had asked for pasta with a simple tomato sauce though, and that was what they were getting.

Because Mike liked giving people what they asked for.

"Wait. Want you in my mouth." Ana's voice came to mind unbidden.

Ah, fuck. This shift would never end.

As the evening progressed, Derek stopped expediting, and worked the floor, trusting Mario to time manage and keep orders organized.

Now he leaned against the pass. "Table 23 wants to see the chef."

Mike craned his neck, but 23 was one of the few tables he couldn't see from his workstation. Eh, it was probably an Italian, wanting to tell him his dish needed basil or something.

"I'm busy." He wiped loose cocoa powder off a plate of Tiramisù and nodded to himself. It looked good. He still had the touch.

"I told her. She said she'll wait."

Her. She. Ana's face flickered in his memory.

Nah. This was stupid. It could be anyone.

"Aren't you gonna ask if she's hot?" Derek arched an eyebrow.

Mike shrugged. It wasn't her. If Ana wanted to see him again, she'd have given him her number.

"If who's hot?" Mario asked. He stopped next to Derek and handed Grant a batch of order tickets, to stick on the rail.

"Table 23?" Mike said.

"Fucking hot, man. Though you should know better than me." Mario winked and ducked in time to avoid a smack on the back of the head by Derek.

So it was her? Or one of several other women Mike had picked up after one of his shifts. "What does she look like?" Mike asked, trying for indifferent.

Mario was already off, a tray of starters in hand.

"You'll find out when you're done," Derek said. "Since you're so *busy* now."

Mike hated the knowing smile Derek couldn't seem to get rid of these days. A steady, happy sex life sure could turn people into jackasses.

"We got a count of six on veal parm," he said, to show how much he really didn't care.

"I'll spread the word." Derek gave him a curt nod, but the smile lingered at the corners of his eyes. He knew something and could barely wait for Mike to find out.

It had to be her.

But Mike should have spotted her when she entered.

He certainly did last night, as did most of the establishment. She balanced elegantly on her high heels; long legs bare under her short, midnight-blue shift dress; hair a golden halo that reached the small of her back. She looked straight at Mike, widened her baby-blue eyes, and licked her lips.

Mike had to stop himself from jumping over the pass and sweeping her off her feet. Then he'd remembered he was working, and she was there for dinner, and he was too old to be ruled by his cock.

The few who didn't see her come in sure noticed when she played with her espresso cup for an hour after she finished her coffee. The kitchen had buzzed with a wager among the waiters on which of them had caught her eye. Mario was everyone's favorite, his dark looks, Italian accent, and effortless charm giving him an edge over competition.

Mike knew otherwise. She stole glances at him all night, and he returned the favor with ever more brazen scrutiny.

When Ana had asked to see the chef, tables turned—so to speak. Not wanting to mess with his buddies' bet, Mike sent Mario to tell her it was a busy night, and unless she had a complaint, she'd have to stay until closing time.

He wasn't surprised when she said she'd wait.

* * * *

Never did a shift crawl by so slowly.

Mike was hyper—chopping, slicing, sautéing, mixing, cooking, plating, and praying for the clock to strike midnight and the kitchen to be closed for food. There would still be cleaning to do, and he was on until one, but Derek would let him at least go talk to—

Ana

—whoever was waiting for him.

Ten more minutes to go.

"I need three espressos and a chocolate soufflé." Mario handed him the tickets.

Fuck. The soufflé needed fourteen minutes in the oven. He was tempted to nuke it, but Derek would murder him if he used the microwave for anything other than decontaminating sponges. The thing was a leftover from when Derek's ex owned the establishment, and she'd driven the restaurant into the ground.

"Grant, you got this?" Mike looked at the cook, who nodded.

Nine minutes to go.

Torture.

At two to twelve, Mike could hold back no longer. He'd already wiped his station and cleaned his utensils—

which he didn't have to do. He took off his hat, checked his white uniform for stains, and when he found none, made his way out of the kitchen. Derek raised an eyebrow but chuckled when Mike told him to buzz off.

Mike could see Table 23 now. She had her back to him, and sure enough, her hair was pale blonde—only shorter. And her shoulders were wider than he remembered.

She turned when he was a couple feet away. "Finally, Mr. I'm-too-busy-to-talk-to-customers," she said. Mirth danced in her blue eyes, as she stood to greet him.

She was gorgeous.

But not Ana.

"*Tanya*." He pulled her in a bear hug, honestly happy to see her. "Your brother could have said it was you."

She grinned. "Derek can be an asshole. Were you expecting someone else?"

Mike's face reacted before he could deny it.

"I see. Flavor of the week, or something more?"

"I don't kiss and tell."

Tanya laughed. "Not how I remember it. Derek kicked your ass when you told people about me and you."

"That was in sixth grade, and it was my first kiss. Of course I told."

Tanya laughed again, and he felt warm inside. She'd been his first love, when he and the Arbore siblings were growing up in New York, but their relationship had evolved into a pure and deep friendship. He always felt better about himself when she was nearby.

"How long are you in town for?" he asked.

"I moved here on Saturday. He didn't tell you that either?"

"That's awesome, Tan."

She took her seat again and motioned for him to join her. "Sit. Tell me how you've been."

Mike sat his ass down and shrugged. "No news here. Work is going well."

"I hear you're cooking again."

"Yeah, I'm—" The rest of that sentence died in his throat, when a gust of cold night air hit him. He had to look at the door.

Ana stood at the threshold, once again looking straight at him, as if she'd known where he'd be.

Even in torn jeans and a loose T-shirt, she was stunning. Mike's mouth went dry, and he was on his feet before he knew he was standing.

Tanya swiveled in her seat, to follow his gaze. "Someone's got a type," she murmured with a chuckle.

"Tan, I—"

"Yup. You got to go. We'll catch up tomorrow."

He rushed to Ana, who was watching him. "You came," he said.

"You're busy."

"No." Mike shook his head. Why did he feel the urge to tell her nothing was going on between him and Tanya? And why couldn't he find the words? What if Ana left before he explained? What if she didn't come back?

Why did he care so much?

"Uh, that's Tanya." He pointed over his shoulder with his thumb. "She's not—"

"I know."

"We're not—"

"I know."

Ana smelled like candy and gazed at him with promise in her hooded eyes. Her lips were still swollen by his kisses. If people weren't watching, he'd take her on the nearest table.

He wanted to tell her she looked amazing. That last night had been the best he had. That he would've called, if he had her number.

He didn't trust himself to make sense, and he knew better than to trust the promises he ached to give, so he did what he did even better than cooking. Mindless of the wolf whistles coming from the kitchen, he slanted his lips over hers and let her perfume steal his breath.

"Let's get out of here," she whispered against his lips.

He'd have to apologize to Derek and the brigade tomorrow.

Chapter Four

She loved and loathed the weird-ass memory dreams in equal measure.

They started the way her actual nights with Mike had, but veered off from there, and she had complete control over them. It was as if she were transported to her past, knowing what she did now.

And what she knew now was that Mike was a two-timing bastard and a liar.

Only she didn't have to hate dream-Mike, like she did her real ex. She could pretend they'd just met, and enjoy their wild time together without worrying about the future. In her dreams, she was free to give in to the animal passion they always shared.

Correction—the animal passion *she always believed* they shared. If he'd lied about loving her, he could've lied about anything.

Last night's dream was one of her favorite memories. In reality, it was their second date. She'd given him her number, and he'd called, and she'd gone to meet him after her recording session.

Her dream had started with her outside *Arbore's*, but she somehow knew Mike wasn't expecting her. She also knew everything else would be the same. He'd be chatting with Derek's sister, and he'd jump up when he saw Ana, and he'd run to her and splutter about who Tanya was.

In her dream, she didn't torture him as long as she had in real life. Back then, Tanya pointed at Mike and then at herself, shaking her head behind his back. Bella realized the other woman was saying she and Mike weren't a thing, but let Mike ramble on for a while, enjoying his floundering.

If Bella hadn't believed him then, she wouldn't have lived a lie for sixteen years.

Her new alarm clock chirped gleefully. She flattened her hand on top of it, and it stopped. Simple as that. Like her marriage.

Why did she keep setting an alarm? With the exception of the lawyer firm handling the divorce, she hadn't really been anywhere since she received the pictures proving she was a fool. She didn't bother with makeup, and on some days, a shower seemed too much effort. Not like she had a job. She could afford to sleep in or be stinky.

She could afford to do many things, now that she was officially due half of Mike's fortune, including his London restaurant. He was extremely proud of the small bistro he'd opened with the money from his first best-selling recipe book and expanded through hours of hard work. Bella was surprised he yielded so easily when she asked for it in the settlement.

"I love you," he'd said. "If it takes losing one restaurant to prove it, then it's all yours."

She took the deeds, but they changed nothing. The hurt and betrayal were still there, every waking moment of every day.

There was no hurt or betrayal in her dreams. She kept her mind off them, as she and the Mike she first fell for laughed and made out at every traffic light on the drive to his place.

"This is me." He opened the door and waited for her to enter. "It's nothing much, but it's quiet."

"I forgot..." How much she liked the sparsely furnished living room that opened to a wide kitchen. Pans and pots hung

from rails over the central isle, and fresh herbs filled the air with their aroma. Her subconscious held on to more detail than she realized.

Mike looked a question at her, and she tried to will away his curiosity. It was her dream; she should be able to control every element. When that didn't work, she peeled off her T-shirt.

In the past, she'd never get caught without a bra. In the dream, her breasts were free to distract him.

They made love on his floor, and then he stood in all his naked glory and allowed her a full view of the sculpted body he still maintained in his fifties, as he walked to the bedroom. When he returned, he had his duvet in his arms. He motioned for her to move to the couch, and when she did, covered her and tucked the edges under her feet. She smiled. She always hated it when her feet were cold.

"I'll make us a snack," he said.

Bella — or was she Ana again for real? — took in every flex of the muscles in his broad back, as he put on his apron. She watched his arms work, while he cut large slices of homemade bread. Listened to him hum a song she no longer remembered the lyrics to, as he grilled the bread, grated tomato, and sliced mozzarella.

And as he plated his creation, drizzled olive oil over it, and decorated the plate with drops of balsamic reduction, she let herself fall for him again.

It was just a dream.

In her reality, in her *now*, she was a forty-two-year-old divorcée, with no future as a vocalist and no tender lover to feed her body and soul.

"Do you cook for all the girls?" she'd asked — in the past and in her dream.

His answer was the same both times. "I've never brought a girl here before."

Both times, she believed him.

If only she hadn't. If she'd laughed and had fun with him, and not returned his calls again, she might be happy now. She might have a career and a husband who gave himself to nobody but her.

There was no going back to sleep. She kicked off the covers and sat up with a huff.

One of the things she missed the most was not having to make her own breakfast. Since they agreed they were exclusive, and except for the five days a month he spent in London, they slept together every night, and he woke her up with breakfast.

She also missed their nightly chats, when she waited up till two, for him to get home and tell her about his day. Her days were usually uneventful, her time divided between the gym, her charity work, lunches with friends, and appointments at the salon.

Oh, God. She was shallow and boring.

Was that what led him to the redhead? Was the girl interesting and intellectually stimulating, on top of young and beautiful?

The sob caught Bella unaware, shaking her chest and ripping out of her throat with the force of her heart breaking. The tears weren't far behind. They poured down her cheeks, soaking the neckline of the shirt she slept in and making it cling to her—warm and sticky and disgusting, like he was.

Like he'd become, because of her?

No. She wasn't to blame for his wandering eye or his wandering dick.

When she met him, she had so much in her life— friends, family, work. She gave everything up, to be with him. Changed her schedule to fit his. Left it all behind, to follow him to London, when Derek made him a partner in the restaurant he launched there. She waited tables at the bistro, when they first opened it, to save him money, and she was uprooted again when Mike decided to return to San Francisco and start a chain based here.

By then, she was Mrs. Mike Zaratino and bound to the responsibilities the position entailed, such as going to luncheons and galas, and being vapid.

She barked a laugh. It was so easy to blame him for everything she'd chickened out of. If she kept on, she might manage to really hate him, instead of going to bed at night craving his touch and praying he'd visit her dreams.

She remembered the first time he took her. How he filled her. How he made her his. She loved the way he moved, whether he was inside her or combining lowly ingredients in the kitchen, to create magic.

Damn it, she still loved him.

This had to change.

Her dreams were a way for her to mend her broken heart, but she couldn't fall down the rabbit hole again. In her sleep, she changed what had really happened into something that suited her more. She was more demanding, less swooning, and definitely not looking for a relationship with Mike. Eventually, she might convince herself to reject him.

If she couldn't break his hold in real life, she'd use her dreams as therapy. It was cheaper than seeing a shrink, and she didn't need to get dressed and face the world.

Her cell rang, but she let it go to voicemail. It would be her mother. Worried. Begging her to reconsider. Bella didn't need another reason to doubt her decision. She needed to get over Mike, forget the past sixteen years, and build a new life that didn't revolve around him.

And she'd start with a shower.

She convinced her limbs to stretch, and grimaced at the ache in her back. It felt like she'd slept on the floor. It might be wise to take up yoga again.

Something caught her eye on the way to the bathroom. The butt-ugly miniature of the Aztec deity sat on Mike's nightstand.

Not Mike's any more. Now it was *the other* nightstand.

Bella didn't remember bringing it to her room, but she had a couple of beers last night, and she was a notoriously lightweight drinker. A shiver ran down her spine when she focused on the statue's painted-on eyes. They were tiny but creepily lifelike. She'd have to move it back to the living room. No way could she sleep there again, with it watching her.

Chapter Five

Two nights in a row was once too many. Mike wasn't the repeat-offender type of guy. One time was all it took to learn everything he needed about a woman, and *everything* was neatly summed up in how good a lay she was.

Ana was an exceptional lay—she could bend like an acrobat—but she'd made him break his rules, and that was dangerous.

Last night he fell asleep with her in his arms, *in his own place*, and he would have spent the entire night with her if she didn't run out. It shouldn't bother him that she didn't want to stay over, but it did, and it showed how close to losing control he was.

And it was all about control.

His parents were still together, still crazy about each other after four decades of marriage, but the idea of losing himself to anyone like they did to each other scared

Mike shitless. No woman was worth sacrificing his freedom, at least for as long as his good looks held.

Which was why he wouldn't sleep with Ana again. Two nights were bad enough, but three would be leading her on, and he might be a total dog, but he never played with a woman's feelings. He created no expectations. He was clear about what he wanted and stressed that he offered no future.

But he *did* ask for her phone number two nights ago.

A momentary lack of judgment. That was all. Alcohol and a great fuck clouded a man's mind. This evening he was dry and thinking straight, and next time Ana appeared, he'd turn her down. Simple as that.

Simpler, with today being a Monday, and him not having to go to the restaurant. He doubted she'd show up at his place. If she were looking for a steady fuck buddy, she'd have given him her digits.

He stretched and rubbed his chest. The skin was tender from her scratches. His cock stirred at the memory of her riding him on the floor, digging her nails into the spot over his heart.

"Oh, give me a break," he told the tent forming in his covers. Thinking of her was enough to make him hard.

This was out of the ordinary too. *Out of sight, out of mind* was how things worked.

He forced himself up and into a pair of jeans and a T-shirt. The sun pouring in the windows called to him. He'd hit the grocery store and then see if any of the guys from the restaurant was up for coffee. With the hours he kept, maintaining a friendship with anyone but his coworkers was next to impossible.

Wait. Tanya was in town, and he'd ditched her rudely. He pocketed his wallet and took out his cell, already dialing her on his way out.

Tanya suggested they meet at the same café Derek had chosen months earlier, to bitch and moan to Mike about Amanda. The irony didn't escape Mike. Last he was there, he'd sat and listened to his boss talk about his impossible landlady. This time, he was the one whining about sleeping with a gorgeous woman. He should have his man card revoked.

"If you like her, why not sleep with her again?" Tanya sounded equal parts curious and annoyed.

"You're not listening. She may think we're dating."

"She won't even give you her number, you jackass. Not all women want to reel you in and make an honest man out of you." She crossed her legs and jiggled her foot.

She always did that when she was upset, but Mike didn't know why she'd be upset now.

"I know. I just don't want her to think that's what I want," he said.

"Because God forbid you actually change your tune when you find a woman worth pursuing." She raised her voice with every word.

"This isn't about Ana and me, is it?" Mike asked.

Tanya huffed. Snorted. Narrowed her eyes. Then she shook her head and let out a dry laugh. "It's not. I'm sorry. I know you're not a dick, and I get that you want to do the right thing. I just don't understand why you think the right thing is denying yourself what you want. You weren't looking for more than a quick fuck—"

"*Tan.*" He looked around. Nobody seemed shocked by the obscenity, but still. "This isn't New York."

She waved dismissively. "Oh, please. People fuck in San Francisco too. You should know. And though you meant to do just that when you met her, things change. If you find yourself at a different place, tell her. Don't be afraid to go after what you want." Her eyes darkened at that. "You never win when you don't try."

Mike reached for her hand. "What happened back home?"

She left her hand in his. "Nothing. I needed a change of scenery, and Derek's place was empty since he moved back in with Amanda. I'd be stupid not to take advantage of a paid apartment by the sea."

"And you're not stupid." He smiled.

"Nope. Not me." But she avoided his gaze.

"I'm here if you want to talk. You know, right?"

Her smile looked fragile. "I know. When I can talk about it all, I'll get a six-pack and pop by your place, like old times."

"You got it."

"Now, when are you seeing Ana again?"

He ducked, his long black hair forming a curtain in front of his eyes and hiding him from Tanya's penetrating gaze. "I don't fucking know."

* * * *

It was that very evening. He opened his door to take the trash to the chute, and Ana stood outside, fist poised to knock.

"Who let you in downstairs?" he asked. It was the first thing that came to mind, and it was stupid, because he really, truly didn't give a flying fuck.

She was there, looking at him with those huge blue eyes and worrying her luscious lower lip with her teeth. "Someone was leaving," she blurted.

Good enough for him. He closed the distance between them, wrapped both arms around her waist, and sealed her lips with his. When she lifted her legs to encircle his hips, he turned and propped her against his open door. Wood slammed against brick, but he ignored it, lost in the heat of her mouth and body.

She twisted a hand in his T-shirt and wedged the other between them, to undo his fly. She didn't mind being taken right there, where anyone could see. Could this woman get any hotter?

She broke the kiss and whispered, "Want you. Now."

He wanted nothing more, but it nagged at him that she seemed to only be after his cock. Normally, he ran from anything resembling a commitment. He never made plans that spanned more than twelve hours with a woman, in fear of getting wrapped up in a relationship, and he definitely didn't turn down no-strings-attached, on-the-spot action.

But he wasn't a life-size vibrator, damn it.

He gave Ana a quick peck on the lips and unlocked her ankles from behind his back.

She found her footing with the ballerina's grace that characterized all her movements. "What's wrong?" she asked. "You don't have somewhere to be."

It didn't sound like a question, but that was probably him. "I was on my way to dinner." An innocent lie. "Care to join me?"

Ana scrunched her nose in dismay.

"What's the matter? Got something against eating?" When they shared the bruschettas he made last night, she didn't give him the impression she starved herself — though she must have sacrificed some things, to have such a flawless body.

"Dinner's fine. I just — this isn't a date, right?"

He was taken aback. "What if it is?" Which it wasn't. It was about getting nourishment and delaying gratification. Nothing more.

"This isn't how it's supposed to be. You call me up, we have a good time, and then I go… back."

Mike frowned. "But I didn't call you. I don't have your number. You showed up here."

She shook her head, her gaze to the floor. "I should leave. I just thought one last night would be fun."

He had no doubt it would, but before he got lost in her body again, he needed to figure out what was in that gorgeous head of hers. "Have dinner with me, and then I promise you all the fun you can manage. Just let me get my jacket." And keys and wallet. And an extra condom, in case they couldn't wait.

She looped her arm through his when he came back out. "So, where are we going?"

"I'm in the mood for Vietnamese. You up for it?" He locked and led her toward the elevator.

She glanced up, eyes narrowing briefly. "Right. I got my nights mixed up."

"Sorry?" Was she bat-shit crazy, or did he hear wrong?

"Nothing."

He probably heard wrong. He called the elevator and kissed her while they waited for it, enjoying how her body melted against his. When the doors opened next to them, she pulled away. Her face was pinched. The woman's mood was more volatile than nitroglycerine.

He was about to ask what was wrong, when she spoke. "Last time we talked was in an elevator."

It was a whisper, but he caught it, and it had nothing to do with him. She'd lost someone. Someone close to her. Maybe her sexual appetite was a coping mechanism. She wanted to forget, and he was nothing more than a distraction. His gut twisted at the thought, but he'd distract her to the best of his abilities.

He pushed her against the mirrored wall and sneaked a hand under her top, to cup one breast. His knee between her thighs kept her in place, while he tasted her lips again. They were made for his, these soft, full lips. A promise always lingered at their corner, even when they weren't arched in a smile.

"Three days in a row," he said, before his brain had processed the words. "You're my longest relationship."

She laughed. "Definitely not a relationship. I won't be making that mistake again."

And once more, words that should have been a reassurance left him aching inside.

The restaurant Mike had in mind was packed, and they got hotdogs and went for a stroll on the pier instead.

Ana bit down on the sausage and let out a moan of delight. "This is better than I remembered."

"How long since you've had one?" Maybe she was a dancer; they weren't allowed junk food.

She laughed. "Eons."

Her laugh was infectious and adorable. He wanted to hear it again. "It's my comfort food," he said.

They walked without talking for a while, enjoying their food, their free hands brushing together. Among the loud throng of people around them, their silence was companionable, not awkward, and when Mike sat on a bench and Ana made herself comfortable with her legs in his lap, it felt like they'd been doing that forever.

He finished his dog and tossed the wrapper in the nearby can. A drop of ketchup had made its way at the corner of Ana's lips. He bushed it with his thumb, and she snatched his hand and sucked his fingertip clean.

Fuck. She was sex on legs, but he didn't want to be thinking of sex now. He wanted to talk. And he recognized the wrongness in that.

"Is your name really Ana?" he asked. Like she'd tell him the truth if she'd given him a fake name to begin with.

"Part of it," she said. She studied his face, and Mike got lost in her eyes again, until the wind sent her long tresses flying across her face, breaking their connection. "My full name is Anabella, but everyone calls me Bella. Ana is the name I use for work. And I give it to guys I don't plan on seeing again."

He should be insulted, but she gave him that lopsided smile he couldn't help but return. "You saw me again," he said.

"I didn't plan on it." She fidgeted with the empty wrapper of her hotdog.

Right. She'd only happened to go by his work and then his home. Something told him pointing that out would make her withdraw into herself. "I'm glad you did," he said, "and I think I'll stick with Ana. I like it."

Her expression darkened. "I've heard so before."

He needed to get the smile back. "Ana, Ana, Banana," he sing-songed.

She laughed. *Score.* "My mom calls me her Banana. My cousin thought that was my real name, until we were six."

"My mom always calls me *Mikey*. When she refers to me as *Mike*—or worse, *Michael*—I know she's about to rain the wrath of God down on me. Used to scare the crap out of me. Now I weather it."

"I know." She ducked her head. "I know the feeling, I mean. When Dad yells *Anabella*, I know I'll hear something I won't like."

"It's funny how they make us feel like kids, even now."

"I automatically turn into a five-year old when I argue with Mom. It was worse when I lived with them. Now—" She paused and scrunched her nose, as if considering something. "Yeah... Now we have lunch together once a week."

Mike nodded. "My folks are in New York. If we were in the same city, I imagine we'd do the same."

"Probably."

"What do you do? For a living?"

The question seemed to throw her. More lip-chewing.

"You don't have to tell me if you don't want to," Mike said. "Or maybe you can't." He let out an exaggerated gasp. "Are you a spy?"

Ana scowled. "Yes. And now that you know, I have to kill you."

They joked more about it, but Mike didn't miss the fact that she didn't answer. They talked until the pier emptied of people. Exchanged barbs about their first time together. Shared anecdotes from their childhoods. And with every little bit of herself Ana divulged to him, Mike's hunger for her grew.

It was more than the insane attraction he felt toward her. Seeing her face light up with mirth and watching her long, elegant fingers move to emphasize her point fascinated him as much as having her writhing against him did. When he mentioned a song he liked, and she sang it with him, he couldn't get enough of her melodious voice.

She said she was up for ice cream, and this time when their knuckles touched, he took her hand in his. It felt familiar. Comfortable. *Right.*

It burned his skin and made his pulse race.

Was this how falling in love felt?

Chapter Six

The smile on Bella's lips disappeared when the harsh light of day hit her eyelids.

The dream was over, and she was back to her stupid, painful reality. Just as well. The dreams got weirder by the night. Having incredible sleep-sex was one thing, but a long, personal conversation over street food? With her ex?

Who'd want to dream of that?

Yes, it was nice watching him hang from her every word, instead of showing off like he really had on their third date, but waking up alone hurt even more than usual.

She squeezed her eyes shut and tried to go back to sleep, long enough to see the end of her not-a-date with Mike. In the real date, they'd gone for ice cream and had sex on the beach, but things might be different in her sleep. Maybe dream-Mike would do or say something to break his spell over her.

And she wanted to be Ana a little longer. She hadn't used that name since she quit singing, but he never stopped calling her that. Ana was happy and carefree and only twenty-six. She was a vocalist, with a couple of great gigs set up for the summer and a contract for her own album just around the corner.

A contract she'd turned down without even mentioning it to Mike, because she wanted to devote her life to him and he'd have urged her to take it.

Bella missed Ana.

"You have an incoming call from *That Fucking Pig*." The robotic voice of her *HouseSsistant5000* boomed over her head. Weird. It used to be a female voice, and Bella had muted it after the fiftieth call from Mike. Probably a glitch in the latest software update.

"Reject," she said. "And set phone sound off."

She was convincing herself to get out of bed, when Mike's voice filled her bedroom. "Please answer me, Ana. Hear me out."

"Reject call. *Reject*." She was going to call WICCTech, the *HouseSsistant5000* provider, and chew them out.

Mike kept talking. "You haven't given me a chance to explain. Someone's setting me up with those pictures."

"Setting you up? Who?" she called out, against her better judgment. "Who has anything to gain?"

He spoke over her. "I don't know what happened."

"Your little girlfriend was tired of fucking a married man, and she decided to take action. That's what happened. No more games, Mike. Stop calling."

"All I know is I love you. I've never loved another woman, and I certainly haven't touched one since I met you. If the pictures are real, if my"—he twisted his mouth—"*lover* sent them, why do it anonymously? Why not tell you when and where they were supposedly taken? Whoever's behind this doesn't want me proving my innocence, but you should know, Ana. You should know. I love you."

She pressed her hands over her ears, trying hard to block out his voice. "End call. *Please.*" She was sobbing again. She'd thought she had no more tears left for him, but here they were, drowning her again.

"End of voice message. Voice message stored," *HouseSsistant5000* said.

A freaking message. At least Mike didn't hear her cry.

But she heard him cry. She heard the catch in his voice, and it tore her up inside. If there was a chance he was telling the truth—

No. Lies. All lies. Back then, and still now. She wouldn't let him trick her again. The pictures were clear.

She remembered the message blinking in her inbox. It had been the anniversary of their first night together, and he always took her to *Arbore's* to celebrate. He'd been waiting in the car for her. He said he loved waiting for her. Loved seeing her always choose to come to him.

She'd seen the notification on her way down the stairs, and pulled up her inbox as she entered the car to sit next to the man she loved, who was supposed to be her home. Her nest.

His hand was on her knee when she opened the message. No subject. The sender was d0wnwf8@dreammail.com. It should have landed in her spam box, but it hadn't. It was in her inbox, waiting to ruin her life. Dread wrapped icy fingers around her lungs and squeezed the breath out of her. She should spam it. Trash it. Report it.

She hadn't. She'd opened it, and looked at picture after picture of her husband fucking another woman. A younger woman. There was no doubt it was him; he faced the camera, eyes hooded, his sensual lips curved in the self-satisfied smile she knew all too well.

"I want a divorce," she'd said. No tears. No waver in her voice.

She was proud of how she handled the situation, not once having an outburst in front of him. No screaming. No calling him names. She wouldn't give him the satisfaction of letting him see he'd destroyed her.

Her mother refused to acknowledge the possibility the pictures were real. Who took them, if they were? Bella had no answer to that, but if Mike was sleeping with another woman, he might have been sleeping with two of them just as easily. One of his horde of lovers might be a photographer.

"You have an incoming call from *Angie*." Her virtual assistant was back to having a female voice.

Bella wasn't in the mood to be pitied, but her cousin had achieved an admirable balance between understanding Bella's pain and not making it the focal point of all their interactions.

"Accept call," Bella said.

"Hi, hon. How are you?"

Miserable, lonely, and beating herself up over her failed marriage. "I'm okay, I guess."

"Should I believe you, or keep asking?"

Bella sighed. "I'm lying, but I don't want to talk about it."

"Okay. Wanna go for lunch? I have a free hour or so."

Bella thought about it. Not like she'd be cooking, and there was only so much takeout she could bury her grief under. "As long as we don't go for Italian."

Angie didn't pretend to find the forced joke funny. "Good. I'll pick you up in an hour."

Bella thought of asking where they'd go, so she could dress appropriately, but decided not to bother. Jeans, a black top, and a blazer would work for most places, and she didn't feel like wearing anything fancier, anyway. "I'll be ready."

Once Angie was off the line, Bella clapped. "Insert memo: Tell Angie about HS issues. End memo and export to cell."

She had to fix the *HouseSsistant5000* before she called Cassandra. She wouldn't want faulty software to mess up something as important as a call to her old manager. This was the only reason she put off calling, not her fear that the woman wouldn't even remember her name.

Cassandra had believed in Ana. She got her the summer gigs Ana was celebrating at *Arbore's*, the night she first laid eyes on Mike. Cassandra had urged her to continue the celebration afterhours, with the hot young chef. Poor woman couldn't have imagined a night of fun would lead Ana to dropping her career and becoming an ornament on Mike's arm.

Bella wanted to blame Mike for her loss. For all her losses. For the wasted years. The more she thought about it though, the more she realized that wasn't the case. She'd allowed herself to be lost in a man. That he ultimately wasn't who he seemed to be was irrelevant.

Maybe she should cancel her lunch plans and try to get some sleep. Then she could dream of being that other woman, who took hold of her destiny and didn't throw her life away for love.

* * * *

"Thought the world's best pork buns would cheer you up." Angie pulled into the parking lot of Bella's favorite Chinese place, and Bella's stomach growled and clenched at the same time. Memories of happier times clogged her throat and made her eyes sting.

Oblivious, Angie checked her rear-view mirror before sliding her car in reverse and easing it into a spot Bella would need a million maneuvers to fit in if her car was covered in lube. Angie's parking was as perfect as anything she tried her hand at, and Bella couldn't help the twinge of jealousy that speared her insides. If she had half of her cousin's determination to succeed, *divorcée* wouldn't be her only qualifier now.

"I said *pork buns*, and you didn't salivate." Angie turned her worried gaze to Bella, her tone too serious for her words.

Bella hoped the smile she managed didn't look pained. "I'm drooling on the inside. Honest."

"I messed up, didn't I? Let's go somewhere else."

Like where? San Francisco was *their* city—hers and Mike's—and they'd made the most of it whenever Mike wasn't working. *Or fucking barely-legal redheads.* He wouldn't kill this place for her.

"I've missed good pork buns." Bella got out of the car, careful not to scratch the Lexus to her right.

Angie nodded and followed suit. "Lock. Alarm set on touch," she said over her shoulder, and her car responded with series of clicks and a long *bleep*.

"This is new," Bella said.

"Prototype. You can set a radius for reaction, and whether you want the alarm to blast everyone's eardrums or text you. I prefer the mayhem option." Angie was the head engineer in WICCTech. She and her wife had established the cutting-edge software company, and both maintained key roles after it went public.

"I like it. Do you have something that repels cheating ex-husbands?"

Angie rolled her eyes and led the way in. "I have some things in mind for him, but I've promised Sarah not to go there."

Bella wouldn't mind talking torture techniques, but she doubted it would help. She needed her mind off Mike.

Angie didn't see things the same way. "How does it feel to be officially free—judge's seal and all?" she asked as soon as the waiter took their order. Her grin didn't reach her blue eyes.

Bella appreciated the effort, but the words sliced through her. "Not as liberating as I expected."

"It hurts, huh?"

"Like a motherfucker."

Angie chewed her lower lip and ran a hand through her shoulder-length chestnut hair.

"Hey. I'll be okay," Bella said.

"I know you will be. It's just so hard sitting back and watching you go through this, when I could— Oh, goddess. I'm making you comfort me? I'm so selfish." She frowned. "And now I'm a drama queen. Ignore me. You talk. How are you feeling? How are you doing? How can I help?"

Bella's smile caught her unaware. She didn't think she had a real one left in her, but Angie's rambling did the trick, and Bella was done hiding. "I'm lonely. I miss him. Can't stop thinking about it all and wondering why I wasn't enough."

"Honey, you can't blame yourself. He's the one who messed up what you had."

"Yes, but maybe he wouldn't have, if I were still the woman he fell in love with. I changed. I lost myself. And I was stupid to believe he'd love me no matter what."

"You weren't stupid." Angie shook her head. "None of us saw this coming. And I'm a friggin' genius; I should have. I still can't believe it's true. I know the pictures checked out, but are you sure you don't want me to look into the email account? I can trace it. We can find out more about…"

The other woman. How not like Bella she was. Or worse, how much she and who Bella used to be had in common. "No. I don't blame her. Mike was the one who swore to love me forever."

The server approached with a tray that held all sorts of delicacies, and Bella and Angie watched in silence while he unloaded dish after dish on their table. Bella reached for the seaweed as soon as the man turned his back.

"You know, there are other things I could do." Angie spoke the words slowly. Carefully. As if they'd break. *Break Bella?*

"Surveillance?" Bella snorted around a mouthful of crispy perfection. "I want to put everything behind me, Ang."

Angie wiggled her fingers, and the tips glowed blue for a split second. Trick of the light? "I wasn't talking about technology," Angie said. "I meant magic. I haven't messed with it since — when did Lexi…? Oh, never mind. The point is I still have it."

It took a heartbeat for the words to sink in. "*Magic?* Angie, it's 2031. Technology *is* like magic, but — "

"No, hon. I'm talking actual magic. I can cast spells." Angie hooked her finger and a spring roll flew into her palm.

Bella gaped. "Is this a new project? A magnet that works on non-metals, or something?"

"Why don't people listen when I talk?" Angie took a bite. "It's *magic*. I have it. Haven't used it since Lexi and Ric got together. Well, not *much*. I promised Sarah I wouldn't meddle with you and Mike, and I thought the statue was enough, but it wasn't, and now I'm thinking maybe I should do something."

This wasn't real. It was another of Bella's messed up, too-real dreams. Her *cousin* couldn't be a witch, and the statue…

"Ugly little Aztec-god guy? You said it was for good luck." Bella's ears buzzed, and shaking her head didn't help, but she did it again. "You can do magic?"

"It was for luck. He is. He's supposed to look after you and make your dreams come true. Not in a horror-movie way. He was supposed to keep you and Mike happy together. Which is why it's so hard to believe he did what he did."

Bella kept her composure. Either Angie was having a psychotic break, or Bella's mind was playing tricks on her, but she'd go along with it. Not like anything else in her life made sense. "You expected your mini-god to brainwash Mike into not fucking anyone else?"

"It doesn't work that way. Xochipilli is supposed to send you good vibes and ward you from external negative influences. It would work if Mike really lo—" Angie snapped her mouth shut so hard, Bella's jaw ached.

"If he loved me."

Angie held her gaze. "I can figure this out. If you want me to."

"Nothing to figure out. What's done is done. And if it's okay with you, I'll forget all you said about magic. My world is messed up enough without more unknown variables."

Angie opened her mouth, seemed to reconsider it, and nodded. "Change of subject. Did you get a hold of Cassandra?"

Not that Bella's lack of a career was her favorite thing to talk about, but it was an improvement. "Not yet. I'll call her tomorrow. Your latest upgrade messed up my *HouseSsistant*. It accepts calls I want to ignore, and the voice keeps changing from female to male. It's a little freaky, hearing a strange man's voice inside the apartment."

"I'll check it out tonight. Remotely."

"Cool. Thanks."

Angie bared her teeth in an imitation of a smile. "And what will you be doing tonight?"

"Um… sleeping?"

"No. You're hot, and you're single. You should be on the prowl."

"I don't think that's happening any time soon."

"Tonight."

"Angie…"

"Tonight." Angie's scowl and the way she shook her index finger in Bella's face indicated she wouldn't drop it.

Bella couldn't win this. "Tomorrow. One drink."

"Acceptable start. And you'll have to talk to a guy. Just one."

Bella leaned back in her chair and shoved half a pork bun in her mouth. Her reluctant nod wasn't exactly a binding contract.

Chapter Seven

"Man, how much salt did you put in that Marinara?" Grant tossed his spoon into the sink with a grimace.

Mike wiped his hands on the towel and grabbed another spoon, to try for himself. Bad. "I can fix it. I'll add some sugar."

"Careful. Don't make seafood marmalade out of it."

"You don't tell me how to fucking cook, all right?"

Grant held up both hands. "I'm joking, Mikey. Don't freak out."

Mike patted Grant's shoulder and forced a smile. "I'm just used to getting it right the first time, you know?" That was why he didn't do second times.

Except for Ana—she broke his rule.

And he wanted her to keep breaking it.

"I got this. You go have a smoke or something." Derek nodded at Grant, pulled on an apron, and tied it behind his back. Grant went out the back, and Derek joined Mike behind the cooker. He sniffed the air over the pot of failed sauce and said, "I can *smell* the extra salt. You're all over the place. It's the blonde, isn't it?"

Mike's first instinct was to tell Derek it was none of his business. Instead, he nodded. He wasn't the kind to talk about feelings and thoughts and relationships, but Derek was his friend, and the rest of the brigade wasn't in yet, so they had relative privacy.

"I've never seen you so discombobulated before." Derek added a pinch of sugar to the marinara and nudged Mike with his elbow. "She's different, huh? Drives you nuts. Gets under your skin. Doesn't let you focus."

"How'd you know?" It was easier to talk when Derek looked at the simmering pot instead of at him.

"Amanda did the same to me. Still does, sometimes. I can never tell what's on her mind."

"Ana—that's her name. She won't give me her number. Says we're good the way we are."

Derek laughed. "You found a girl who doesn't want commitment, and of course you get hooked."

Mike crossed his arms over his chest. He felt defensive, though his rational mind said Derek wasn't attacking him. "It's not like that. I'd want her—" He wouldn't finish that aloud or in his head. "I don't want her because she's not looking for a relationship. I just... I like her. We have fun. She's smart, and she's funny."

"And good in bed?"

Mike clenched his fists until his knuckles hurt, to keep from planting one of them in Derek's nose.

"I see it's not like that." Derek turned to face him, his blue eyes serious. "If you like her, why not date her?"

"Are you deaf? She won't let me."

"Did you tell her that's what you're after?"

Mike thought back to his too-brief, sex-filled nights with her. "Not in so many words, no. But she brushes me off when I mention anything about future plans."

Derek widened his eyes in mock horror.

Mike punched him this time, but it was light and on the shoulder. "You're a jerk. I mean arrange to meet up for coffee. In advance. Like people do."

Derek returned his attention to his cooking. Added some olive oil. Pepper. Tasted it again. "Maybe she doesn't do plans?"

Or maybe she didn't want to do Mike again.

Maybe she was already *doing* someone else. She didn't want Mike calling, because another man might pick up the phone. The man she went home to, after Mike fucked her. The one she woke up next to.

The possibility sent a stab through Mike's gut. "I need a break."

"We haven't started yet."

"Just gimme fifteen. You got this." He had to get some air, put his thoughts in order, and think of what little he knew about her. Maybe he could find her?

"Go. Fifteen minutes, man. I'm serious."

* * * *

Times like this, Mike wished he still smoked. He could sure as fuck use the high. He could bum one off Grant, but he refused to pick up the habit again.

He shoved his hands in his pockets and kicked at an empty bottle. At Derek's orders, the alley behind *Arbore's* was kept clean, but the cleaning crew wasn't due for another hour. The heat had gotten to the trash, and the smell of rotting food assaulted Mike's nostrils. He didn't want to be here. He wanted to be with Ana.

A rundown minivan sputtered his way, and the front wheel landed in the single puddle of water in the entire alley. The puddle that was right in front of Mike.

"*Hey.*" Mike's pants were drenched in muddy water, the shittiness of the situation matching his mood.

The minivan stopped, and the driver hopped down, followed by a cornflower-blue mist. No—not mist. It was glittery.

Whatever.

"Did I get you, buddy?" The man was several inches shorter than Mike and had a foreign accent. His pale-blue eyes were haunting against his tanned skin. "I'm sorry. Didn't know the thing was there."

"You wouldn't, would you?" Mike wanted to be pissed off, but the man's smile lightened his mood. "Anyway, this isn't the worst thing to happen to me lately."

The man nodded and gave a knowing smile. "Girl-trouble, huh? I know about that."

"Yeah." This was a weird conversation to be having with a stranger. "She doesn't see me the way I see her."

"She will, if you let her."

"That was vague and useless."

"I'm good at vague." The guy laughed. "Anyway, if it's true love, it's fated."

It was an odd thing to say, and Mike was about to point that out, but the man climbed back in the mini and shut his door. The huge-ass sign on it read *Willy's Moving Solutions.*

Mike raised his gaze and caught a flash of blonde hair on the minivan's mirror. *Ana.*

Willy — or whoever the guy was — probably thought Mike's was crazy when Mike took off after the woman who rounded the far corner of the restaurant.

"*Ana.* Ana, wait up," Mike called out.

The woman stopped, turned, *and it was her.* Mike waved like an idiot and closed the distance between them. "I didn't think I'd see you again."

She narrowed her eyes.

Was she upset? Had he fucked up? "Ana? Is everything okay?"

"Do I know you?"

His heart shuddered and skipped a beat. He searched deep inside for what he hoped was a charming smile. "I sure hope so. You seemed to, last night."

She recoiled like he'd slapped her, and then took a tentative step back. "What?"

"This isn't funny. Did I do something wrong?"

Her second step back tugged at his gut, adding to the burning inside. Was she afraid of him?

He held up both hands. "I'm sorry. I thought we had fun together. Didn't mean to scare you." He turned to go but stopped and faced her again. He couldn't leave it at that. "Please tell me what I did wrong."

She shook her head. "I have no idea who you are." She looked around, eyes wild. "You can have my purse. Just don't come closer." There was utter lack of recognition in her gaze, as she slipped the strap of her bag off her shoulder.

"No. *God*, no. I'm not robbing you. We" — how to put this? — "went out a couple times. I thought I made more of an impression. Unless… do you have a twin sister?" It was worth a try.

She shook her head again, looking only marginally less like a deer caught in the headlights.

"Well, okay." He huffed, to keep from screaming. What was wrong? Was she sick? Dying? Was some horrible disease stealing her away? "I have to go back to work. Can I give you my number? Maybe we can go for coffee some time. Talk about… stuff."

She chewed on her lip. "When did we go out?"

At least she didn't tell him to fuck himself. "Last night and the night before. And the one before that."

"Saturday. Last thing I remember that night was partying. Here." She tilted her head toward *Arbore's*. "I woke up in my bed, alone, and my manager told me I passed out and she carried me there. But I didn't drink."

"I remember."

"You were there?"

Shit. This was going to be hard to explain. "I work at the restaurant. We left together. Pretty late. But you weren't drunk."

Her chin trembled. "What did we do?"

Could earth open and swallow him whole, please? "You... We... It was consensual. I swear."

Ana shook her head. "I didn't have sex with you."

"I'm sorry."

"No, this isn't denial. I didn't have sex with you. I woke up fully dressed. Not even a little bit disheveled. And I'd feel *something*, if we had. An aftermath. I wasn't hangover. I'd know."

The idea she was under the influence of some drug their first time together dug a hole in his chest. "We should take you to a hospital. Have a blood test. See if someone slipped you something."

She laughed. "Yeah, I'll get in your car. Will you give me candy, too?" Defiance had shoved aside fear, and the knot in Mike's stomach loosened a fraction.

"It wasn't only Saturday, Ana. Maybe you're sleepwalking or something, but you've come to me. Three nights in a row." He reached for her arm without thinking, and she batted his hand off.

"Listen" — she made a wide gesture that encompassed all of him — "*guy*. Whatever you think happened, didn't. I was in the recording studio all day Sunday. Till three in the morning. I couldn't have been with you. Now I'm going to take a long nap and forget all about you. I suggest you do the same, because I have enough crazy in my life already."

She had enough crazy? "Ana —"

"Stay away, or I'll call the cops."

She was off, and he was left wondering what the fuck just happened.

It wasn't the last time that day.

When Mike took out the trash at the end of the night, Ana waited outside the back door in a flowing pale-gray dress that made her look like an angel. Hope blossomed in his chest, but he extinguished it. "The cops with you?" He'd made it through his long, *long* shift by convincing himself she meant nothing. He couldn't allow her to pull him back in.

"What do you mean?" She frowned. "I can't remember this."

There they went again. He wouldn't sit back and let her do her thing this time. "Like you didn't remember me this afternoon?" he asked.

She looked shocked. "This afternoon? But I didn't sleep."

"What does that—"

Slashing an impatient line in the air with her palm, she asked, "Where did you see me?"

"Right here. I chased you down. You said you didn't know who I was, and to leave you alone."

Her breath came in short bursts, and he could see the whites of her eyes all around the irises. Panic. He'd caused it.

This time she let him touch her. Grab her by the arms. "What's wrong with you? Is it your head? Or was someone watching earlier? Are you hiding?" *Please be hiding, and not crazy.* He pulled her closer. "What are you afraid of? Fucking tell me."

She met his gaze and held it. "You, Mike. I'm afraid of you and all you'll do to me."

He dug his fingers in. He couldn't help it. Pain and worry and disgust at himself for scaring her poured out of him in a wave. "What *I'll* do to you? You're haunting my days. My work is suffering, because I never know if the last time I saw you is the fucking last time I'll fucking see you. You were supposed to be a quick lay in a club restroom, and I can't stop thinking about you.

"I want to taste you. I want to hear you moan. Make you laugh. I want to bury myself inside you and live there. And I don't even fucking *know* you. I don't know your last name or where you live or what you do. All I know is you fuck like a demon and you have my nuts in a vice. And this afternoon I was nobody to you. Don't tell me I scare you, Ana. You fucking petrify me."

She grabbed his T-shirt and shoved him back against the door. It felt familiar and yet new. Her lips found his, and she cupped him over his jeans. "Forget you? I've tried so hard. For months. I wish I could."

She was crazy.

And he was lost.

Chapter Eight

Stop thinking. Now. Feel this.

Where did that thought come from?

Mike was kissing her, and she was kissing him, and she didn't care that nothing was as it should be in this dream.

He was supposed to come outside, give her a kiss that turned her knees into jelly, and take her for a moonlight stroll. Then, of course, there'd be sex. There always was, when they were in close proximity. What wasn't supposed to happen — what shouldn't happen — was for her to be kissing him and crying, and praying she never awoke.

"Ana, please tell me what's wrong." Mike pulled away long enough to search her face with his gaze. "Whatever it is, we can fix it."

They could, in this dream-world. She could believe him again, and he could love her once more. Or convince her he did.

"What you said. All of it... I came out of a hard relationship. Bad."

He clenched his jaw, his mouth set in a hard line. "If he hit you —"

"No. Nothing like that. We were together for a while, and I always put him first. I gave up my dreams for his, and he slept with someone else. I guess you remind me of him." She was explaining herself to a figment of her imagination. To the shadow of a memory.

But that memory had his hands buried in her hair, and his warmth spread through her body. "I'm sorry." He sounded like he had on her voice mail, this morning.

Sixteen years from now.

"Not your fault." Not yet. If she could stay in the dream, not ever. They'd kiss and fuck and make love and be in love forever. If she didn't hate drugs, she'd get a prescription for sleeping pills, first thing in the morning.

"Hey. I'm not him. I'd never hurt you." Mike folded his arms around her, and she buried her nose in the crook of his neck.

It wasn't a lie yet.

It'd be easy for her to write him off as an asshole, who played her from the start, but he loved her back then. Maybe not on their fourth date, but soon. And for a while. She didn't know when things fell apart, but it wasn't when his eyes were hooded and his fingers burned and his heart thudded against her chest.

Stupid, detailed dreams.

She lifted her face and found his lips again. Soft but demanding, they pressed against hers until she opened up to him with a sigh. "I'm not him," he told her, mid-kiss. "I'm yours."

She remembered the first time he said the words. And what came next, if she didn't shut him up. "No more talking. I want you." The first time around, she wore leggings. Her dream-dress was much more convenient. She bunched it up and raised one leg over his hip.

Mike grasped her thigh and lifted her. She locked her ankles behind his ass, and he turned, to pin her against the alley wall. He smashed his mouth to hers again, anchoring her in place with one hand, as he yanked down her neckline and freed her breasts with the other.

"Do you want to stop?" He didn't seem to realize he was grinding against her. "Go somewhere else?" He kneaded one breast, and Ana thrust out her chest.

"Here," she half-said, half-moaned. Reaching between their bodies wasn't easy, but she managed to pop his fly and wedge her fingers inside his pants.

"Wait. We need a condom."

"We're both clean, and I'm on the pill."

He didn't ask how she knew about him. He used his thigh to prop her up, and withdrew enough to pull out his cock. He all but tore the skirt of her dress from her hand and slipped a finger inside her. "God, you're so wet."

"I said, no more talking." She closed her fist around him, drove her hips forward, and impaled herself on his shaft. She watched his face, as his eyes slid shut and tension seeped away from his expression. For a moment, he seemed ecstatic.

When he looked at her again, wild desire burned in the depths of his brown eyes. He slammed inside her with the same hunger he had their first time. He didn't lower his gaze, and it spoke volumes. It promised her the world.

She didn't want this to be a dream. She wanted to be twenty-six again, and jumping into love – head first and hope intact.

The connection was there. Electrifying. Consuming her at the same time it filled her with life.

Bella snapped awake in her huge-ass bed. The sheets were tangled around her legs, drenched in her sweat, and her pussy throbbed. Her heart ached.

She couldn't go back to him. Ever. This was supposed to be taking him out of her system. Instead, she was falling for him all over again, and knowing how it was all going to end hurt her more.

She needed to talk to someone, figure out the ball of yarn that was her psyche, and stop the dreams, or she'd never move on.

The statue of Xochipilli mocked her from her nightstand. Her cleaning lady must have brought it to the bedroom yesterday, and Bella hadn't noticed. She should move it somewhere else, but if she did, it meant she believed Angie. That she believed in magic.

Its eyes were still creepily intense.

"What are you looking at?" She reached to turn it away. It felt warm under her fingers.

* * * *

She hadn't been out for a drink in a long while, but bars hadn't changed much in the past couple years, and neither had men. A handful approached her, but although she appreciated the attention, she didn't spare them a second glance.

Except for the sinfully hot blond watching her from two tables over. His blue eyes were striking against his bronzed skin, and unruly curls crowned his head. His strong nose and square jaw kept his lush lips from looking too soft, and his wide shoulders hinted at a muscular physique she wouldn't mind seeing more of.

Angie would be proud of her for noticing.

The man smiled and raised his glass, as the waiter placed a strawberry daiquiri in front of Bella.

"From the gentleman over there." The waiter tilted his head toward Mr. Hot.

She smiled and nodded at the stranger, who stood, drink in hand.

Uh-oh. Wrong move. She didn't remember how to flirt, and she wasn't interested in going home with someone. Even a someone as tall and well-built as him. And *young*. He looked no older than twenty-five. She sucked a long gulp of the pink drink, enjoying the icy slush as much as she did the alcohol kick.

"Mind if I join you?" Even his voice was gorgeous. Deep and smooth, like a caress. Before she could blurt a lie about waiting for someone, he pulled out the chair next to her, sat, and leaned back with an easy smile. "Drinking alone depresses me, but I'm only in San Francisco for a night, and the hotel room was stuffy."

In town for one night and out for some fun. He might help her blow off some steam and get her mind off Mike, but it had taken her an hour to talk herself into getting out of her sweatpants this evening. She'd need at least two weeks' time, to decide whether to sleep with him tonight.

"Thank you for the drink, but I'm not looking for company," she said, avoiding his gaze.

"Even if I promise I'm not here to hit on you, convert you to polytheism, or otherwise bother you? We can sit, finish our drinks with or without talking, and then I'll be on my way and leave you to whatever is eating you up."

She sized him up with a frown. "What's in it for you?"

"I'm a writer. People are where I get my inspiration, and I believe there is a story in you. If you decide to share it, it'll make my night more pleasant. If not, I'll still have the pleasure of sharing a drink with a gorgeous woman."

Come-on lines had improved since her time. *Vastly* improved. "I'm about twice your age. Besides, I thought you weren't going to hit on me."

He chuckled. "I'm not. My heart belongs to another" — his phrasing made her smile; a writer indeed — "and I'm *much* older than I appear."

"An old soul?" The smile lingered. This talking-to-new-people thing had merit. He wasn't looking at her with the pity she saw in the eyes of friends and family.

"You can say that. So will you share your story?"

She shook her head. She didn't want her past to define her tonight. Her black pencil skirt and pearl-white silk shirt made her feel sexy, and she wanted to enjoy the lie while it lasted, not revert to the betrayed, bitter woman who woke up from dream after dream of her treacherous ex-husband, aching for his touch. "Will you share yours?" she asked.

Mr. Hot swirled the amber liquid in his glass, and she thought she saw cornflower-blue sparks in it. They matched his eyes. "I met her several lifetimes ago," he said. "It was love at first sight, but I was an idiot. Instead of telling her how I felt, I went with a grand gesture that backfired, and then I was petulant about it. She hates my guts now, but I still believe we're meant to be."

"That doesn't sound deluded at all."

"Right?" His laugh sounded like clinking crystal. "The thing is, she turns me down and then looks for excuses to see me. She says she doesn't want me, but she steals heated kisses in the candlelight. I try to keep my distance, and she's everywhere. It's messed up." He ran his fingers through his hair.

His eyes looked older than the rest of him for a minute. Ancient and all-knowing.

Alcohol was doing a number on her mind.

"I know all about *messed up*," she said.

He raised his glass. "To *messed up* and second chances and *meant to be*."

"I'm sorry, but this is a load of crap." The female voice sounded so close, Bella jumped in her seat.

A waitress leaned in to leave a bowl of cashew nuts between them. "There is no destiny, and second chances only lead to more heartache."

Her long chestnut hair only allowed Bella glimpses of her face, but she looked familiar. Bella tried to get a better look, but the waitress swiveled away, saying, "If he's hurt you, he'll do so again, unless you don't let him."

The woman was rude to interrupt, but her opinion echoed Bella's. "She does have a point," Bella said. "Maybe you should let go and start over with someone new." As should she.

Mr. Hot—she should have asked his name—followed the waitress with his gaze, his jaw set and his lips pressed into a thin line. When he returned his attention to Bella, he was smiling again, but his eyes were filled with sadness. "Inside every cynic beats the broken heart of a romantic," he said. "It was nice meeting you, Anabella. Now if you'll excuse me, I have an early morning tomorrow."

Bella was left watching his broad back, as he made his way through the tables, toward the exit. How tipsy was she, that she introduced herself with her full name and didn't remember doing so?

Eh, perhaps one more drink would help keep the dreams at bay. She really didn't want to see Mike tonight.

Chapter Nine

Mike's shift had been over for an hour, the restaurant was closed, and he still waited by the front entrance.

Like a lost puppy, waiting for its owner.

It drove him mad that Ana made him feel this way. Correction—that he felt this way. It wasn't her fault. She wasn't the one who got his hopes high.

But after last night…

Their coupling had been as fierce as ever, but she'd seemed more *present*. She'd held his gaze as he thrust inside her, until her eyes slid shut with her release. He'd seen her very core, and she was as into him as her was into her.

So why wasn't she here?

Did he scare her away?

He rounded the block, to see if she was by the kitchen entrance. Not that she'd be waiting there. If she wanted to see him, she'd find him. Plus, he'd already checked a couple times.

She wasn't coming.

And he was an idiot. She was probably at his place, wondering why he wouldn't answer the door. *That* was why people had cell phones, damn it. He should have asked for her number again.

Part of him wasn't surprised not to find her waiting outside his building. He lay awake until sunrise, hoping the doorbell would ring and she'd be there, to fill his apartment and his heart with her unique essence.

Ana never showed.

A ringing woke him up, but it was his phone. Some guy asking if he was interested in a new cable-TV offer. Mike bit back some choice words and ended the call.

His sour mood followed him to his shift and splashed all over his performance.

"Table 12 returned the Puttanesca. Too spicy." Derek all but dropped the plate on the bench.

"It's meant to be spicy." Mike tossed the food in the trash.

"But not like it's been spewed out of hell—which is how they described it."

Mike shrugged. "Lightweights. If they don't like my recipe, have Grant do it."

"Someone's in a bad mood."

Mike looked at the blond busboy on the other side of the kitchen pass. "What was that?'

"I said you seem to be in a bad mood. Cooking is all about love. If you're pissed off, the food's no good."

Mike had never seen him before, but the way the guy's blue eyes glittered was familiar. Mike should tell him to shut the fuck up and mind his own business, but he had some time to kill while Grant remade a perfectly fine dish. "Maybe I shouldn't be cooking today, then."

"It's about a woman, isn't it?" The guy folded his arms on the pass and rested his chin on them. "Is she amazing?"

Derek snorted. "She must be, if he's such a mess."

"Don't you have a restaurant to run?" Mike asked.

"Tuesday night, man. Dead," Derek said.

Mike turned to the busboy. "Yeah, she's fucking amazing, and she's gone AWOL on me."

"What did you do to her?"

"Nothing. We clicked. She's got her issues, and she won't talk to me about it." Why was Mike explaining himself to a stranger?

The busboy straightened and slapped one hand on the countertop. "Don't give up, man. If it's true love, it's fated."

Who the fuck said anything about love?

"Should I skip the red pepper flakes all together?" Grant asked.

Mike turned to tell him to do whatever the hell he wanted, but a hint of blue made him spin back to where the busboy stood. The guy was no longer there, and Derek stared wide-eyed at the space he'd occupied.

"Did you hire a magician or something?" Mike asked.

Derek shook his head. "Wasn't my hire. Thought you knew him. Gonna check the cash register. The fuck is going on? Anyone can walk in from the street and pretend to work here?" He left in a huff, while Mike tried to make sense of what happened.

The blue eyes. The sparkles. *If it's true love, it's fated.*

Maybe Ana wasn't the one losing it.

* * * *

"Want a ride home?" Derek asked.

Everyone else had already left, but Mike had stayed behind, to prep for tomorrow. He hated being off his game. Hated more that it was because of a woman. "Nah. I'll walk."

"It's chilly outside." Derek pulled the door shut after him and locked.

"I know, *Ma*. I've got my jacket."

Derek shrugged. "Suit yourself. Maybe the cold night air will flush the asshole vibe out of your system."

"Fuck you." Mike glared before he caught the hint of a smile on Derek's lips. "Sorry. I'm just—"

"Hating the taste of your own medicine. Got it."

Fury crawled up Mike's throat, choking him. "You don't know what you're talking about." But he wouldn't be this angry if Derek was wrong.

"I've seen you blow girls off time and again after a single night. The only reason this one drives you nuts is you didn't get to show her the door first."

"This isn't— She hasn't shown me the door." Should Mike be focusing on that instead of on his friend's opinion of him? Both made his blood boil, and he let his frustration with Ana and his anger at Derek mingle into a single, menacing entity.

He shoved his fists in the pockets of his jacket, afraid of what he might do if Derek provoked him. "Don't act like you have your shit together. A year ago, you were mopping about your ex stealing your restaurant. Everything you have now—*Arbore's*, Amanda, all of it— was a stroke of fucking luck. Don't pretend you have all the answers. If Amanda hadn't broken off her engagement for you, you'd be chasing after tail and taking no names, like me. Hell, that's what you meant to do with *her*, at first."

Derek narrowed his eyes. "It's different with Amanda."

"Because you've got her. She snapped you out of your self-pitying haze."

"And you think Ana can do the same for you." Derek studied his face, gaze filled with an understanding that wasn't there before.

Mike snorted. "Hey, I never needed saving." He just needed Ana.

"If you say so." Derek shrugged. "You sure you wanna walk?"

"Yeah." Better not to be in an enclosed space, with his current mood. Derek would say one thing, Mike would understand another, and he might end up without a job or a best buddy. "Need to stretch my legs."

"Not like you've been standing all day." Derek's chuckle sounded fake.

Mike's was no more genuine. "Right." He waited till Derek was in his car, and then took off toward his place. His stride wasn't hurried. He didn't want to get home, only to see Ana wasn't there again.

Was Derek right? Was Ana's hold on Mike the fact that she kept leaving? Her face came to mind, flushed with the force of her orgasm, her eyelids half closed and her lips parted. He wanted to wake up next to that face every morning. Always.

"*Fuck.*" His voice echoed like a gunshot in the quiet of the small hours. He ducked his head and walked more briskly. All he needed was for someone to call the police on him.

Think. He had to think of a way to find her. He knew her first name, and she said something about a recording studio. When he'd run into her on the street, she was going for a nap. On foot. That meant she either lived or worked near the restaurant. He'd ask Derek for the footage of the twenty-four-hour security camera that covered *Arbore's* front. If Ana passed by frequently, he might be able to track her down or arrange for another *chance* meeting.

Assuming she wasn't outside his building now, waiting for him.

She wasn't.

Mike didn't feel half as devastated as the night before. He had a plan now, and if he had the balls to admit to himself that he was in love with her—and he was, damn it—he'd manage to fix whatever was keeping her away from him.

Chapter Ten

Bella thought not dreaming of Mike would make her feel better. She was wrong.

She woke up tired, but without the sweet ache between her legs or the satisfied tingle on her fingertips. And she was lonelier than ever.

She'd flirted with guys the night before, though nobody as handsome or interesting as the mysterious blond. It hadn't gone past a few smiles and compliments, because she wasn't looking for more. She wouldn't have gone further with Mr. Hot either, if he'd pursued her.

She was done with Mike, but her heart hadn't gotten the message. It ached for him. Her body did too. It was empty without him. Cold in his absence. Purposeless.

Was punishing his indiscretion worth all this pain? He swore he was innocent. That he was framed. It made no sense, but maybe he'd only done it the once. Should she forgive him?

No.

Leaving him had nothing to do with punishing him for sticking his dick in another woman—though taking his London restaurant might have been a little about that. It was about protecting herself from more betrayal.

Her heart and her body would have to get used to being without him. Eventually the numbness would cover the pain. Maybe, if Angie really could do magic, she could help Bella forget.

But not yet. Bella wanted to dream of the man Mike used to be one more time. One more night with him might be enough.

She hated lying to herself.

"You have an incoming call from *That Fucking Pig*."

Damned *HouseSsistant5000* refused to block his calls despite Angie's fiddling with it. And it still wouldn't change back to the female voice.

"Reject," Bella said.

"You may want to hear him out."

What the hell? Was she still asleep, or did the friggin' software offer her relationship advice?

She clapped her hands. "Uninstall *HouseSsistant5000*." Some problems needed radical solutions. Mike was one of them, and another night with him would solve nothing. It would only add to the pain of a decision already made.

"Uninstall *HouseSsistant5000* in progress. Are you sure you don't want to give Mike a second chance? He may be telling the truth."

Or he might have managed to tamper with the program. He was the one who'd installed it, to begin with. Why couldn't he leave her in peace—allow her to sweep him under the rug, drown him out, and continue her lonely existence without doubting her sanity?

Bella all but ran to the bathroom and under the shower jet. The roaring of the water masked anything else her fucked up electronic assistant had to say, but it didn't mute her thoughts or the memory of the toast the gorgeous stranger made last night.

She slipped down the glass wall of the shower and curled into a ball. She wound herself tightly around the hollow space in her ribcage and promised to protect it at all costs. There would be no second chances. Mike wasn't her *meant to be*.

She had a life to live, and she'd start by meeting with Cassandra and working on her career.

She got out of the shower, wet but not clean. She clapped her hands and grimaced at the quiet. It would take some getting used to, but she could function without a digital housekeeper. She turned on her TV and linked her phone to it, before bringing up the browser. Having to do things herself instead of relying on her electronic assistant was odd, but she'd been around before the thing was invented. It'd come back to her.

Bella looked up Cassandra Orare, not hoping for much; she didn't know if her old manager remained in San Francisco, or was even still in business. She couldn't believe her luck when the single result listed an address in Inner Richmond, where Cassandra's office used to be.

Good. Awesome. She'd call Cassandra first thing in the morning. Or put it off, in lieu of more wallowing.

Bella chewed on her bottom lip. If she was going to start over, she needed to take the first step. "No time like the present." She dialed the number on the screen and prayed Cassandra remembered her and was magnanimous enough not to hold the past against her.

"Cassandra Orare."

Shit. The phone didn't even ring. Cassandra should have an assistant. Why was she answering her own phone? Bella wasn't prepared for this. And she wasn't talking. Why wasn't she talking? She had to say something.

"Hello?" Cassandra said. Her voice was the seductive purr Bella remembered.

"Umm... hi." Bella wanted to smack herself for sounding like a child. "Hello, I mean. I don't know if you remember me. I'm" — who was she? — "Anabella Matthews. You were my manager a million years ago."

"Anabella Matthews? I don't — *Ana? Is that you?*"

Relief burst a capsule of adrenaline in Bella's veins, at the same time the name — *that was Mike's and would always be Mike's and it fucking sliced her up and it hurt to hear* — brought a sour taste to her mouth. "You do remember me. Hi." She'd said that already.

"Of course. I forget nothing. What's happened to you? Are you a rock star in Europe by now?"

"I wish." Bella laughed. It scratched her throat.

"Japan?"

"No. I'm not a star anywhere." The words cut irrationally deep. "I haven't sung in a long while."

"You gave up?" There was something beneath the surprise in Cassandra's voice, and it wasn't pleasant. Sounded too much like satisfaction.

"Yeah. Should have known better. And how are you? Still in the music industry?"

"Darling, it's lovely to hear from you, and I'd love to catch up, but I'm with a client."

That was polite as far as brush-offs went. "No, I completely understand. Sorry I bothered you."

"Hush. It's no bother. I simply can't talk right now. How about drinks tonight? Come by my office. We'll chat."

"Really?" Shrill and desperate. Not the best way to enter a business relationship. Bella cleared her throat. "Sure. Is eight good for you?"

"Eight will be perfect. Do you have the address?"

"I do." Bella tapped her screen and copied the address, to send to her GPS.

"Good. See you then. And this time we'll make you a star."

It might be the right time to point out she was forty-two and out of practice, but Bella wouldn't push her luck. "Can't wait."

But she had to, and the day seemed to draw longer, just to spite her.

By the time she reached Cassandra's office, she'd changed in and out of three outfits, and felt like she stank, despite two showers and tons of planet-friendly deo. She was buzzed in as soon as she identified herself, and spent the elevator ride regulating her breath, to calm her nerves.

When the metal doors opened to Cassandra's smiling face, the knot in Bella's stomach loosened. It'd be all right. Even if Cassandra didn't take her on, Bella would keep fighting. A decade and a half of pampering herself and working out meant she looked years younger than she was, and her current misery had slimmed her lithe body to within showbiz parameters. She had another chance, and she wouldn't squander this one.

"*Ana.* It's like time stopped for you. You look gorgeous." Cassandra clasped Bella's shoulders and gave her an air-kiss on each cheek.

Cassandra looked exactly the same as she had sixteen years ago—not a single line marred the skin around her intense blue eyes, and her jaw line and cheekbones were as sharp as ever—but if Bella said so now, it would sound insincere. She settled for saying, "You should talk. You're stunning."

Cassandra stepped back and waved away the compliment. "Great beautician. Better plastic surgeon. You wouldn't believe the miracles you can buy these days." She looped her arm through Bella's and pulled her toward an open space with leather couches. "Tell me everything you've been doing since I last saw you. Start with why on earth you'd give up singing."

Bella let out a nervous laugh. "Got married. Divorced now. You don't need to know more about that."

"Oh, but I want to." Cassandra motioned for her to sit, and then moved to the fully stocked bar by the bay window. "Drink?"

"White wine, if you have it."

"I have almost everything, darling." Cassandra's gloomy tone didn't match her words. She returned with two glasses of wine, handed one to Bella, and joined her on the couch. She kicked off her designer pumps, folded her long, stockinged legs under her, and said, "Last thing I remember, you were giving up what would have been an amazing career, to follow a hot guy half around the world."

And wasn't that the root of all her troubles? "That didn't pan out."

"I'm amazed you expected it to. At the time, it sounded so ludicrous, I was convinced it was a lie. For years I believed a record company had bypassed me and snatched you up. When I didn't see you climbing the charts, I realized you were probably telling the truth. I assumed you started over in London. That was where you went, no?"

"It was, but I was too busy helping my husband — boyfriend then — realize his dream, to have time for mine." Bitter? Her? Nah…

"Typical. And now that his midlife crisis destroyed your marriage, you're back here, to grovel for my help."

Bella recoiled. She knew things had been too easy. Cassandra wasn't planning on taking her on. "I'm merely evaluating my options. And you're apparently not among them."

"I'm sorry. That was insensitive. It still stings that I offered you the world and you turned it down for a man."

"You're exaggerating. I was a vocalist, not a lead singer." And he wasn't just a man. He was her Mr. Right, and she'd been utterly taken with his dark-brown eyes and his shaggy hair that kept falling in his face. Bella smiled, but her heart wasn't into it. She sipped on her wine, relishing the burn down her throat. It was sweet, with honey undertones. She usually went for dry, but the promise of a buzz that came with this was soothing.

"You could have been much more. You *will* be much more." Cassandra leaned closer, and her eyes seemed to grow, filling Bella's field of vision. "Tell me, what do you want?"

Mike.

A do-over.

To un-know the truth about her marriage.

Mike.

Bella bit back the first few answers that jumped to her lips, and said, "I want a career. I want to do what I love and to be good at it, and I want people to know."

"This is all still about Mike, isn't it?"

The wine was stronger than Bella thought. Her head throbbed, and Cassandra's eyes swam with stars.

Bella brought a hand to her head. "I shouldn't drink on a empty stomach."

"I'll have something brought to us, and then we'll set about building a new career for Ana Matthews." Cassandra rubbed her hands together, and Bella's vision focused again. Cassandra's excitement reminded Bella of a puppy's.

Overexcited puppies are unpredictable.

Such a weird thought.

With her head a bit clearer, Bella said, "I wanted to talk to you about changing my name. I go by Bella now."

"Oh, no. That sounds so... common. You're *Ana.* Yes, I think we'll even drop your last name. Plus, a comeback is easier than a reinvention. I can sell that. We'll start recording on Monday. I have to make sure you've still got it, but I have faith in you. I could book you on a tour. Nothing big. Opening for Justin. He's making a comeback too. His fifth."

Cassandra droned on, but Bella only registered parts of her grand plans. She tried to make sense of Cassandra's eagerness to help her. Was the woman that desperate for a client, or did she see something in Bella that Bella herself couldn't? Bella didn't dare hope it was the latter, though Cassandra had made good on all her promises last time they worked together.

Bella had been one of her first clients. Maybe Cassandra liked the challenge of picking up where they left off—and under harder circumstances. Or she wanted to take revenge for Bella leaving her high and dry back then. No. She sounded committed to making things work. She wouldn't be holding a grudge over something so stupid and after this long.

"I'll work for my standard commission, of course. Oh, it will be so much fun working with you again," Cassandra said. "You'll forget all about Mike in no time."

Twice.

Huh?

It took Bella a heartbeat to catch up with her subconscious. Cassandra had mentioned Mike by name. Twice.

"You know my ex-husband?" Bella asked.

"I wasn't hiding under a rock. I know about his restaurant chain. You landed a good one." Cassandra winked. "Too bad he couldn't keep it in his pants, but it's his loss, right?" She tilted her head toward Bella's glass. "You don't like the wine?"

Bella gulped down the contents of her glass and held it out to Cassandra. "I think I need another taste." And the years of her marriage wiped from her memory.

Chapter Eleven

Derek slapped his hand on the bench. "Mike. Focus. I'm trying to be understanding here—we've all dealt with heartache—but you're dropping the ball."

"I've got it." A week without feeling Ana's flesh against his should have helped Mike forget her, but it only made the ache deeper. Not seeing her, not being with her, felt *wrong*. Like his life wasn't supposed to be this way. Like every night without her carved a fresh tear in his heart and led him more astray.

"Like hell, you do," Grant yelled in his face. He was usually so easy going and eager to help that his outburst threw Mike for a loop.

"What did you say to me?"

"I said you ain't got shit. This woman's allergic to nuts, and you put crushed walnuts in her salad. The fuck's wrong with you?"

Ana. Not-Ana. The lack of Ana was all that was wrong with Mike's life, and it made his pulse race and throb in his temples. "Watch your fucking mouth." It was all he could say to Grant. Not like he had a logical argument for why his focus and his cooking had gone to hell in the days since he last saw her.

"Cut it out. People can hear." Derek snapped his fingers at them.

"Whatever. He's a liability" — Grant indicated Mike with his thumb — "but it won't be me dealing with the lawsuits if he keeps it up." He turned to his workstation, shaking his head in disgust.

Mike ought to redo the fucking salad without fucking walnuts and keep his fucking mouth shut, but he fucking couldn't. "Yeah, you heard your master. Tuck tail and run away, like the little bitch you are," he said.

Derek rounded the pass and wedged himself between Mike and a seriously pissed-off Grant. "Grant, you take over the kitchen. Mike, with me." Derek pulled Mike out the back by his sleeve, and slammed him against the outer before the door closed behind them. "Get your act together. I can't keep covering for you."

"Didn't ask you to." Mike's inner voice hollered for him to stand down, accept he'd been acting like an asshole, and ask Derek for time off, but if he didn't have his job, he had nothing. Cooking was the only thing that took his mind off Ana, however temporarily. If Derek took it away, Mike would be left staring at his walls, wallowing over could-have-beens… instead of doing so in the restaurant kitchen.

Derek leaned close and spoke slowly. "This is my business, Mike. You're like a brother to me, and family comes first, but I'm still one installment away from paying off the restaurant, and I'm not gonna let you screw us both over because you didn't get the girl. Sometimes you don't get the girl, and sometimes the girl is a bitch."

Mike swung at him. He'd never hurt Derek before, and he didn't realize when he raised his fist, but a second later, his best friend since childhood was on his ass, looking up at him with a mix of fury and pity.

"You hit me," Derek said.

"You shouldn't have called her a bitch." Mike held out his hand.

Derek took it and climbed to his feet. "I shouldn't have. I just hate what this is doing to you. Stay home a couple days. Get drunk, punch a wall or ten, and snap out of it. Grant can hold the fort till you're back, or I'll find someone else for a while. You can go back to managing." He chuckled. "Where you can't poison anyone."

Mike gave a half-hearted smile. "Two days. Then I'm back in the kitchen."

"You get back to normal, the kitchen is yours till Nicholas is back on his feet."

Mike nodded. "Sorry for that." He pointed at Derek's cheek.

"Yeah. I'll take it out of your paycheck. Pray Amanda doesn't come after you, for messing with perfection."

* * * *

Mike jumped in the shower. The water was near scalding, the way he liked it. Anything cooler wouldn't rid him of the kitchen smells—cooked oil and garlic and spices and everything he fried or seared or let simmer throughout his shift—that soaked his body and seemed lodged inside his nostrils.

Ana said she loved how uniquely *his* the combined scents were.

Thinking of her had an instant effect on his body. He closed his eyes and leaned against the fogged glass. He ached with need for her, but his touch would have to suffice. He closed his hand around the base of his cock and squeezed. He dragged up his fist and slid it back down, twisting his wrist. Water wasn't the best lubricant, but he didn't shut it off, relishing the heat on his chest and arms as much as he did the pressure on his shaft.

He tugged at himself again, recalling Ana's face when she went down on him at the club restroom, heavily made-up eyes turned up at him, her mouth stretched around his girth.

He pulled harder.

The next time, at his place, he'd buried his face between her thighs. He could taste her now, as he stroked faster. He thrust his hips against his hold, barely mindful of the slippery floor of the shower stall. All he cared about was coming, but it seemed just out of his grasp without Ana. He redoubled his efforts, unwilling to accept her absence affected something he'd excelled at since his early teen years.

What finally triggered his release was the memory of her on his couch, smiling that thousand-watt smile at him. The rare one, of pure joy, which held no trace of a hidden sorrow.

Mike opened his eyes, to watch his cum spray the glass in strings. The water was going cold. His insides matched it.

He needed Ana.

Chapter Twelve

"That guy is totally checking you out." Cassandra nudged Bella with her elbow and raised her glass to the handsome stranger at the other end of the bar. "You have to unwind once in a while." She'd taken it upon herself to fix Bella's love life, but they'd had this conversation at least ten times in the three weeks Bella had been back in the studio.

It grated on Bella's nerves. "I'm fine. I'm not looking for a man," Bella said through clenched teeth. She gave the man a polite smile and turned away, hoping it was enough to convey her lack of interest. When she glanced his way again, his appraising stare made her feel exposed in her shiny, low-cut top. She felt like letting him know she wore pants beneath that. This time she shook her head before giving him her back.

San Francisco had kept its timeless appearance, but most bars now were well lit and sterile and served alcohol-free concoctions and bio-something-or-others, that were meant to prolong life but made Bella feel ancient. The bar across the street from the recording studio had character. The lighting was low, the music was loud and from before her time, and the patrons belonged to a decade she was more familiar with.

Cassandra smiled at the man over Bella's shoulder. "Come on. He's the millionth guy you turn down. One of them has to be your type."

"I appreciate your concern, but last time I listened to you and jumped a guy, I ended up here." Bella softened the words with a small laugh, but Cassandra winced.

"I didn't tell you to marry the guy. *Any* guy. Certainly not this one." She indicated Bella's would-be suitor with a subtle tilt of her head. "They're all backstabbing assholes in the end. That's why you take what you need from them and run."

Bella wanted to ask if that was what Cassandra did and how it felt being single at fifty, but she took a sip of her white wine instead. A tiny, dark, petty part of her was glad Cassandra was alone too. Guilt clawed up her throat, and Bella drowned it with another swig of her wine. Other than her ill-advised suggestion years ago, Cassandra was the only one Bella knew without a direct link to Mike, and their nightly girls-drink after recording was a soothing new constant in Bella's life.

Bella rubbed her naked ring finger. "If we're ever going to finish this album, I don't want any distractions."

And she felt dirty at the thought of a man other than Mike touching her. Ironic, considering he'd probably taken things up with his young mistress. He hadn't called in a week.

It might have something to do with her changing her number, when she moved out of their apartment and into a loft closer to the studio, and warning everyone she knew against giving him the new one.

Fucking *Mike*, always on her mind. Maybe she should give this guy a chance. She pretended to check her phone, and glanced at him through her eyelashes. Dark hair and eyes. Wide shoulders. Strong jaw. Nice smile. He cradled his drink in palms almost as large as Mike's.

But he wasn't Mike.

"I'm tired," she told Cassandra. "Think I'll go home." She stood and reached for her wristlet.

Cassandra frowned. Her midnight-blue eyes darkened to black, and her mouth twisted for a second, before settling into a sad smile. "You okay to walk?"

"It's not that far, and I'm not the one who's drunk half a bottle." Bella gave her a quick hug and walked out, memories weighing down her feet. She hadn't just lost Mike, but her sense of being. Wiping him from her life left her avoiding those closest to her. She didn't call her parents, and even Angie had stopped trying to see her after that lunch.

Mike haunted her favorite *everything*, and Bella had to relearn to exist without him. Were things even a fraction this hard for him? Did he ever lie awake at night, hating himself for fucking up?

God, she wished —

No. Dreaming of him wouldn't help when she was finding her balance.

But maybe one last night…

Why would it hurt?

He was inconsequential to her *now*, but he'd be a respite from her loneliness. She yearned to feel whole again. Safe. Loved. Like she belonged.

Seeing the face she loved so devastatingly and those eyes that radiated love before they became another reminder of his deception. Feeling his rough palms, the calloused fingers mapping her skin. Opening herself to him. Having his weight on top of her, pressing her to the mattress as his heat reached her core.

Bella wanted it all, just one more time.

She was on the right track, finally. Pulling her life into shape, and shifting her focus away from Mike and toward building a career. Dreaming of the past—a different past, where she was aware of what came next, instead of giving in to the whirlwind of emotion—posed no threat to her now. She wanted one time. One last breath of him. One more taste, to tide her over.

She pushed her keycard down the slot by her door and let herself into the place she now called *home*, that felt anything but. The new furniture was supposed to signal a fresh start, it but was too modern, too strange… too not her. Glass and chrome and a tiny kitchen fit only for boiling pasta for one and reheating TV dinners—which oddly survived as an institution through the years.

Mike had no place in here.

Bella crossed the open floor space to her bed and flopped on the mattress. Not too hard, not too soft. Perfect and yet not hers. Her place felt no more familiar than a hotel room. Her clock blinked on the nightstand, bathing the ugly small statue that stood in front of it in an eerie red glow. She'd taken the figure of the little Aztec god with her as a joke. A mock-tribute to the good-luck powers Angie thought it had. Maybe it worked; it was a small miracle that her agent took her back after so many years and worked to put her on the map.

And hadn't she left the statue on the coffee table? She remembered thinking how out of place it looked there — out of *time* — and that she liked the inconsistency.

Her eyelids felt heavy. She should change into something more comfortable. Take off her makeup. She was too old to go to bed like this and expect her skin to thank her for it. And she should lose the boots. They'd been a smart purchase. They looked the rock-star — wannabe — part, but were as comfy as trainers on the walk here.

She'd close her eyes for just a second, and then get up and get ready for bed.

God. She wished Mike would be waiting for her when she went to sleep.

She leaned against a cold wall, her naked shoulder pressing into the rough brick. She didn't remember getting here, which meant she was asleep, and the telltale signs of that kind of dream were there. Her surroundings didn't have the flimsy quality of worn-out memories. They were drawn in stark relief, punctuating details she was surprised she'd noticed, let alone retained. Bella had her bearings, she was several years younger, and she knew without a doubt that she was waiting for Mike.

That he'd come to her.

As if thinking of him conjured him, Mike rounded the corner. He was lost in thought, his hands deep in the pockets of his jacket, his gaze on the ground his boots ate up. Bella ached to close the distance between them, but took the opportunity to watch him unobstructed.

His hair hid his eyes, but the jaw line she saw was hard set. His jacket was open, and the T-shirt he wore stretched against his sculpted chest. His jeans hugged his long legs.

As she focused on his face, he looked up and met her gaze.

Fuck.

She could still lose herself in those eyes. Always would. She wasn't over him. She would never be over him. His mouth twitched, and his lips curved into a smile that lit up his face.

Bella's heart skipped a beat.

He quickened his stride, until he was almost running.

She was disappointed when he stopped in front of her, instead of swooping her up and mashing his mouth to hers.

He studied her face for too long, before he spoke. "You came."

"I couldn't stay away."

The gentleness with which he closed his arms around her surprised her. He didn't press her body to his, didn't dominate her with his wide frame, but held her like she might break and scatter in the wind.

He buried his face in her neck and inhaled deeply. "Come home with me," he whispered.

Here, now, she didn't have to say no.

Chapter Thirteen

Even as he held her, he couldn't believe she was there. With him. Holding his hand in the elevator and giggling when he laid kisses all over her face.

"You came," he said again. He sounded stupid. "I'm glad."

"I didn't know if I could. If I should." A shadow darkened her baby-blue eyes.

"Why?"

"Mike—"

"You're married." He didn't care if she was. Marriages ended every day, and if she was with Mike now, she wasn't happy with her husband. Mike would show her she was meant for him and him alone. For the first time in almost a month, he didn't feel the sense of wrongness that permeated everything in her absence.

"No. Not anymore," she said.

He tangled his fingers in her hair and turned her to him. "Good. I don't want to share you." He ached to bury himself inside her, but greater than his desire was his need to know her. To break through her defenses and uncover the mysteries she hid at her core. He wanted to make her his as much as he was hers.

She strained against his hold, so she could slant her lips against him. "There's no one else. There will never be anyone else for me."

Her words should make his heart soar, but the finality in her tone scared him. Was he right before, about her being sick? Was life so cruel that it'd throw love in his path only to snatch it away again?

The car came to a stop, and the doors slid open. Ana pulled him outside before he could ask what was wrong. Her laugh echoed fake in the corridor, but he wouldn't pressure her to open up. She was here, and she'd talk when she was ready. And Mike would listen.

They didn't get farther than his living room before clothes and pretenses were discarded, and their bodies melded together. Mike felt like a dork for spending more time caressing her face than cupping her ass, but he guessed that was what being in love did to him.

Their joining didn't hold the fervor their last time together did, and yet it lacked none of the intensity. Their lingering looks, their languid touches, were lined with desperation. Mike knew his came from fear of losing her again, but what was Ana desperate for?

Her eyelids fluttered, and she looked at him with such yearning, the answer was obvious. Ana was desperate for him.

After sex — lovemaking? — he pulled her close, her back to him. Her heartbeat echoed in his ribcage.

"I'm happy," she said. "Didn't believe I could be happy again."

He didn't want to ask the question, but he had to. "You really loved him, huh?"

She stiffened but nodded. "My dad picked me up from school one day, and on our way home, we saw a black cat lying on the side of the road. He'd been in a fight, and he was bloody. A mess. My dad tried to approach, to see if he could help the poor guy, and the cat hissed. He seemed feral, but his eyes held pain. I was six and not afraid of anything. I knelt in front of him, ignoring my dad's warnings, and the cat stretched his neck, to sniff me.

"I stayed there, until he got up and rubbed his length against my knee. He left blood all over my favorite tights, but I didn't care. I gathered him in my arms, and he went lax. Like that was where he always wanted to be. I must have squeezed too hard, because he scratched me — more a reflex than to hurt me — but I didn't let go. I carried him home and nursed him to health. He hated everyone else, but he was my cat until he passed away from old age, years later."

She turned to look at him. "I never told anyone this, but" — she paused and chewed on the inside of her cheek — "my ex-husband reminded me of that cat. Like he was feral at heart, but he was at home with me. When I got the pictures of him with another woman, I couldn't believe it."

She'd told Mike someone hurt her, but he'd assumed it was a boyfriend, not the man who'd promised to share his life with her. Anger choked him at the bastard who'd broken her heart. How could any man have Ana and ever want someone else?

He wanted to tell her again he wasn't that man. Mike would never hurt her. Never betray her trust. Never not love her enough to be true.

He wanted to tell her he loved her — madly, completely, devastatingly. This wasn't the time, though, so he kissed her, and then he kissed her some more, and then he spent hours showing her body what he couldn't say out loud.

The early morning sun was finding its way through his living room curtains by the time he was satisfied he'd erased her ex's memory from her skin.

Ana lay on her side and trailed her fingers through the sprinkle of hair on his chest. "Where do you go when I'm not here?"

Her question made no sense, but he answered anyway. "Nowhere. To work. Maybe a beer with friends."

Her smile was sad. It made him fidget.

"I'll make us breakfast." He kissed her knuckles and sat up.

"You don't have to." She sounded drowsy, and her thick eyelashes were heavy with sleep and the exhaustion that came from multiple orgasms.

He shouldn't let that go to his head, by the way.

"I want to," he said.

"You don't get it." She closed her eyes and lay back, her pale hair fanning around her like a halo. "I won't be here when you get back. I'll be where I have to be, and you'll go where you go when I don't dream you up." She was mumbling, probably half asleep and talking gibberish, but an icy finger slid down Mike's spine.

He laughed it off, unwilling to let anything harsh his afterglow. "You're not going anywhere. I'll lock up, and you'll stay here, and we'll have breakfast." And they'd talk more, and she'd fall in love with him, and they'd start doing all the sickeningly cute, couple-y stuff he used to make fun of before Ana walked into *Arbore's* and stole his heart.

He felt stupid for actually bolting the door, but he told himself it was to keep bad elements out, not his lover in.

Snippets of their talk the night before came unbidden, to haunt him, as he scrambled eggs and thickened them with heavy cream. Ana's ex had driven her to Mike's arms, but Mike couldn't find it in his heart to be grateful. No wonder Ana acted like she didn't want more than casual sex. She was scared of going through the same shit again. He wanted to find the guy and wring his two-timing neck.

Before Ana, Mike's heart had never run the risk of breaking, because he'd always kept it well hidden. And because he made sure the only part of him that formed attachments to women was his dick. With Ana, he was plunging head first in the darkness and hoping he didn't crash and burn. She was worth the risk, but would she come to feel the same about him?

He spooned the eggs on a large plate and garnished them with parsley and homemade salsa. He put the plate on a serving platter, added a sliced-up ciabatta—buttered—and hand-squeezed four large oranges into two glasses. A rose would look good with that, but he had no flowers at home, and a sprig of thyme wouldn't have the same effect. No problem. He didn't need to go the whole nine yards with the rom-com clichés.

"Breakfast is served, my lady."

The lack of answer made his gut clench, until he saw her sleeping form.

Of course she was still there. Where could she go?

He left the platter on the coffee table and knelt to pick her up. As he carried her into his bedroom, he was struck by such a strong sense of déjà vu, he nearly lost his balance. He steadied himself and continued to his bed. Ana rolled to the side the moment she touched the mattress, and he climbed in behind her.

Screw breakfast. He was too tired to eat, anyway.

He wedged one arm under her head, and she scooched closer. "I'd missed this," she mumbled. "Our bed felt empty without you."

She thought he was her husband. Mike should wake her up and take her again, to remind her whose body she was snuggled against. His chest hurt, and he realized he'd stopped breathing.

"Love you, Mike," Ana whispered.

He didn't care if he never took another breath.

Chapter Fourteen

The freaking alarm clock was getting on Bella's nerves.

"Oh, shut up," she said.

The thing kept making that annoying sound. Of course it did. She hadn't spent the extra thirty for the voice-controlled feature. She reached out to turn the thing off, but her open palm made contact with something completely different than the flat surface she expected.

Something warm and yielding, that moved when she dug probing fingers into it.

A face. A man's face, judging by the stubble.

Bella kept her eyes shut, as she went over last night in her head — her actual night, not the one in her dream.

She'd gone home alone after her drink with Cassandra, as she always did. She hadn't invited anyone over. Did someone break in and drug her?

Sure. And then he tucked her in, rolled over, and went to sleep.

But this had to be it. The only other explanation was well above her usual level of everyday crazy.

She cracked open an eyelid and saw a too-familiar ceiling – that wasn't her own.

No. This wasn't possible.

A glance to her left revealed Mike, watching her. He was grinning, and her hand was still on his cheek.

"Good morning," he said.

She recoiled so hard, her ass slid off the mattress, and she had to grasp his arm to keep from falling on the floor.

"Is my morning breath that bad?" Mike pulled her closer and tucked her hair behind her ear.

"You can't be here." She couldn't, either.

"This is my place." He frowned, but his eyes sparkled with mirth.

Bella sat up and pulled the covers with her. "I can't be here. I can't wake up with you."

His face fell. "Is someone waiting for you at home? You said you were divorced."

"I am. God. This isn't happening." She had to wake up. This wasn't her life. Never before had her dream continued after sunrise.

"Dog? Cat? Kid?"

"Huh?"

"What do you have back home, that you shouldn't spend the night?"

"Nothing." She had nothing worth going back for, and for a second, she entertained the possibility of staying here and starting over with Mike. Righting their wrongs from the first time around. Being herself within their marriage, instead of just Mike's wife.

What if this wasn't a dream?

She remembered their tryst behind his restaurant a lifetime ago, in this version of her past. If this wasn't a dream, there was another Ana here. One who never met Mike and never got to sample his all-consuming brand of love. Bella didn't know if she pitied or envied her, but she couldn't replace her.

"Do you have to go now? Have coffee with me first. Maybe finally give me your number?"

She shook her head. "It won't do you much good. We can't have more than this, Mike, and I don't even know for how long. It's never lasted this long before."

"And here we go with the cryptic shit again. I wish you'd just talk to me. Tell me the truth. Whatever it is, it can't be worse than not knowing if I'll see you again." He sat up and dropped his head back, to land on the headboard with a thud.

This was a dream, and she'd wake up eventually. Which meant she had the luxury of talking to him about the insanity of their situation, without worrying she'd end up in the loony bin.

"Remember my ex?"

He snorted. "Hard to forget." He shook his head. "I'm sorry. I ask you to open up, and then I'm a jerk. Thinking of how he treated you grates on my nerves. I'm sorry."

"Yeah, well, he's you."

Mike arched a brow. "I told you before, I'm not him."

"But you are. You're him, sixteen years ago. For me. You're him now for you." And could she make less sense than that?

"Am I going to need a smoke for this?"

"Probably. I think you still have a pack in your nightstand. Second drawer."

Yes, let's scare the man.

"And you know this because…" He seemed remarkably composed, which meant he didn't believe her.

Who cared?

"Because we were together for sixteen years. I even lived here with you for a while, before we got married."

He fished his cigarettes out of the drawer and put one in his mouth, but he didn't light it. "And that happened when?"

Bella sighed. "Let me take this from the top. In my reality, I'm forty-two — "

"You're holding up well." He sounded nonchalant, but she knew him better than that. The tightening around his lips and the way he rolled and unrolled one corner of the sheet

129

betrayed his nervousness. For all he knew, she was a psycho who'd attack soon.

But she'd be gone soon. "I met you when I was twenty-six, almost exactly the same way we met this time. A couple months later, Derek made you a deal. He looked to expand overseas and wanted you to go to London. Head the restaurant there as his equal partner. I came with you. We got married, and you wrote a cookbook and then several, and opened your own restaurant there. In my present Mike Zaratino's chain of restaurants is everywhere." And she now owned the first one, because he deserved to lose it.

"I thought we were happy," she said. "That you were happy with me. Then... You know. You never owned up to cheating, but we got a divorce. And I've missed you since. So much that I dream of you, some nights." She caressed his cheek and was relieved when he didn't withdraw from her touch. "I dream of us like this. Back when it was all about the sex and the love and the fun. It hurts when I wake up alone, but I always wake up alone. In my bed. Sixteen years from now. After you broke my heart."

He let the unlit cigarette fall and kissed her inner wrist. "So this is dream."

Was it this easy? Did he believe her?

"This isn't real." He threw the covers off the bed, exposing their naked bodies, and rolled her nipple between his fingers.

Bella arched into his touch, and he wrapped his other arm around her waist and pulled her in his lap. His cock was hard between her legs. He brought his mouth to her neck and worried the flesh there with his teeth, as he lifted her by the hips.

Bella tilted her hips, and led him inside her. Her cunt was still sore from last night and protested the intrusion, but his lips on her neck and his thumb on her clit made up for the discomfort.

He thrust with his hips, and she slammed hers down, to meet him. Again. And again. And again. Until her head was light. His fingers dug into the flesh of her ass. Probed lower. He coated a digit in her sleekness, where their bodies were joined, and pressed it to her puckered hole.

Bella bucked but didn't resist. The pressure increased until he slid the finger inside her. Not one finger. Two. Burning and stretching her to the threshold of pain, as his cock pounded in her pussy. She didn't control her body, and she didn't care to. The buildup of her orgasm rose in waves, drowning out everything but pleasure.

"Tell me this isn't real. Tell me my cock is a memory. That it's not drenched in your arousal," he whispered against her skin.

"You don't believe me." Unsurprising, but it pissed her off, so she rode him harder.

He pulled her head back by her hair and sought her gaze. "I believe you believe it. But I am real, Ana. I am real, and I'm not going anywhere."

She was, though.

She came apart around him and pulled him after her. What he thought didn't matter. None of it mattered. In the morning – her morning – it'd all fade away.

She flopped on the mattress next to him and threw an arm over her face. "It was all real once. And you loved me." She didn't mean to sound sad.

"I still do." He covered her face with kisses. "I love you, God help me. We'll figure this all out. I'll prove we are real, and we can be so good together."

She wished he was right.

He gave her ass a playful swat and stood. "I'm going to get that breakfast I owe you, and then we'll talk some more."

"Okay." If she was still there.

She focused on staying awake, but the clanging of pots and pans from the kitchen turned soothing, and before she knew it –

Bella opened her eyes, panicked, but it was too late. The stark-white walls of her loft greeted her. She was fully clothed and above the covers. Alone.

She swallowed down the tears that threatened to spill from her eyes. She wasn't a love-struck girl. She was a grown woman, and she refused to cry over something she lost forever ago.

She got out of bed and took off her boots. Her body felt sore and sated, and the memories from last night played in her head in Technicolor. Mike's body. On top of her. Beneath her. Inside her. He'd kept saying this was real. That he was real, and with her.

The dream didn't feel like a dream. None of them did. But what were they? Surely not time travel. She lived in reality, not a romance novel.

She went for a quick shower. All that talk about breakfast, and she still hadn't had any. She'd go out. Maybe call Angie, see what she and Sarah were up to.

She forgot to remove her makeup before showering, and when she stood in front of the sink, her eyes were sticky with mascara. Technology had progressed by leaps and bounds, but Bella wouldn't consider permanently dying her lashes or getting sparkly inserts like fashion dictated.

She lathered her face with makeup-removing foam and pressed the button for the mirror to heat up and defog.

When she raised her gaze to her image, it felt like an electric current ran her through, straightening her spine and making her toes curl.

She had a hickey where Mike nibbled and sucked on the sensitive flesh of her neck. Somehow, she'd carried it through the barrier that separated dream from reality. Through a timespan of sixteen years.

Her dreams weren't dreams, and deep down she'd known for a while.

"*God.*" What was happening to her? Was she living a parallel life with Mike? Was she losing her mind?

She got dressed and returned to her bedroom, thinking of the statue on her nightstand. She *had* placed it in the living room. She never brought it by her bed. Whenever she dreamed of Mike — or visited him, or whatever the hell took place in her sleep — she'd made a wish for it. And every time, Xochipilli was in the room with her.

Watching the chubby little figure as if it would move to attack her, she said, "I wish Mike never cheated on me."

She didn't know what she expected. That the last few months of her life would rewind and fast forward again, to a different outcome? Nothing happened.

"I wish Mike still loved me as much as he did when we got married."

She berated the small part of her that wanted to believe in magic and wishes coming true. She huffed and fished in her purse for her phone. She'd call Angie. Not about magic, about breakfast.

But maybe she'd mention the dreams and put her cousin's problem-solving genius to work.

The downstairs buzzer echoed through the large room, and she checked the screen by her door, to see a painfully familiar face.

Mike.

Bella's heart skipped a beat. Had he followed her to her present? Her brain caught up to what her eyes had already registered—the shorter hair, the red-rimmed eyes, the haunted look. Not the young lover who couldn't have enough of her, but the ex-husband who wouldn't accept they were done.

She pressed the intercom button and said, "I don't want to talk to you."

"I'll stay here until you let me in. I love you, and I have no problem yelling it for the whole world to know." The words were slurred. Had he been drinking since he woke up, or hadn't he gone to bed yet?

Not her problem anymore, but she didn't want her entire building knowing her business. She buzzed him in and wrapped a scarf around her neck, hating herself for caring what he'd think about her hickey. Then she opened the door and leaned on the doorframe. He wouldn't come inside. There was no place for him in her new life.

When he showed up, he stank of alcohol. It wasn't like him to drown his sorrows, but that wasn't her problem either.

"Why are you here?" she asked.

"When I couldn't find you, I went crazy." Gone was the composed man who tried to reason her out of signing the divorce papers. Mike was disheveled, desperation etched on his gaunt features. "I can't live without you. I can't *be* without you. I don't know how."

Hearing him echo her feelings chipped at her resolve. *No.* She hadn't chosen this; he'd forced her hand.

"Then you shouldn't have slept with someone else. Don't you see you made a lie out of everything I believed in?" A sob made it up her throat and out of her lips before she could compose herself. She hated showing him this weakness.

"I never touched another woman. Haven't given anyone a second thought since our first kiss. How can you not know this? How can you not know *me*?"

The pain in his eyes sliced right through her. He was such a good actor, holding her gaze while he spewed lies.

"I thought I did," she whispered. "Please go, Mike." She moved to close the door, but he grasped her wrist and pulled her flush against him.

"Don't do this to us," he said. "Someone framed me. I don't know this woman. The pictures were doctored. That's not me."

"Angie analyzed them. They're real." It took all of her willpower to push away from him, but he wouldn't let go.

Instead, he tangled his fingers in her hair and buried his face in the crook of her neck. "There is no one else. There can never be anyone else. If you send me away, you condemn us both to a life without meaning."

He nuzzled her cheek, and despite knowing better, she let him guide her mouth to his. Their lips touched, and electricity coursed through her veins. It would be so easy to step back inside with him and shut the world out of their bubble. To build a cocoon and lose herself in him again. To no longer pretend she could exist without him.

He deepened the kiss, thrusting his tongue between her lips, and she had a vivid mental image of him shoving his tongue down a young redhead's throat. The smell of alcohol was overpowering, but it wasn't what brought bile rising up her throat.

This time she managed to break free. "If I stay with you, I condemn myself to a life of doubt. I can't, Mike. I'm sorry."

Bella returned to the safety of her glass-and-chrome palace, and watched the intercom screen until she saw Mike exit. His kiss still burned her lips.

She glanced at Xochipilli one last time, before she called up Angie's number on her phone. "I wish… I wish I knew what to do, to be happy."

Chapter Fifteen

Mike searched his place for the millionth time. He even went through his cupboards and drawers, as if Ana was a misplaced wallet, not a woman who disappeared from a locked apartment.

He'd come back from the kitchen, to ask how she wanted her coffee, and she wasn't in bed. She wasn't under it, either—he checked after he couldn't find her in the bathroom or the balcony.

Not in the closet. Not in the fridge. Definitely not in the top drawer by the cooker. The front door was still bolted from the inside, and Ana hadn't jumped out the window. She'd merely vanished, as had her clothes from his living-room floor.

At least she wasn't naked, wherever she might be.

He should do something. Call someone. The police?

And say what? That a woman he'd slept with a few times left without a trace? He didn't even know her last name. How had he fallen so hard for someone he barely knew?

Fuck.

The feeling of uselessness was overwhelming. Out of options, he unlocked the door, threw it open, and called out her name. No response.

He had no way of finding her and nothing to do with his day. Minutes earlier, he was in heaven. Now despair weighed down his shoulders and addled his brain.

What she'd said... Could any of it be true? Well, it was *her* truth, but could it be real?

Great. He was actually entertaining the possibility his future ex-wife had travelled back in time for — What? His cock? He was damn proud of the thing, but it wasn't worth disproving the laws of physics.

Ana had some mental disorder, and he had to decide if he cared enough to stick by her and help her battle it. If she allowed him the choice.

If she was really sick and knew so much about him, could he be in danger? Shit. All the hot ones were crazy. Derek could attest to that; his girlfriend had been cuckoo for a while. But she hadn't been a stalker who thought she could time travel.

Mike should count his blessings that Ana didn't try to kill him in his sleep, and he should forget about her.

And yet he couldn't stop thinking of her.

He called Tanya for advice, but she was getting ready for a job interview and couldn't talk. All the guys he knew were either at work or still asleep, in preparation for the evening shift. He needed some deadbeat friends, for mornings like this.

He tried to watch TV, but nothing held his attention for more than a few minutes. His mind kept wandering back to Ana, to the nights they shared... to her freaking cat, even. He channel hopped until his stomach grumbled, and then he threw away the two trays of ignored breakfasts and made lunch.

Being here without her felt wrong, like his reality was molded around Ana, and now she wasn't here, the spots she used to occupy hovered just out of sight.

Stupid, senseless thought. This was his apartment, and she'd been here two—three times? *His* space. She'd visited and left. No reason for Mike to feel bereft.

But he did. And when there was a knock on his door, he knew it was twelve minutes to midnight, because he'd been checking his watch every so often.

He didn't look through the peephole. He knew it was her, and he let her in and held her while she cried. When she clung to him, her body wracked by sobs, he had his answer. He'd stay by her side, come what may. Ana was his future.

They stood in his doorway until she quieted. "I'm sorry," she said. "I managed not to cry all day, but seeing you..." She shook her head.

He led her to the sofa, and they curled up together. "Do you want to talk about it?" he asked.

She sniffled. "Why? You already think I'm crazy."

He should deny it, but he couldn't lie to her. "So what have you got to lose?"

"Nothing, I guess. Best case scenario, if you're a creation of my subconscious, you may help me make sense of it all." She straightened and turned to look at him. "I saw you today. The other *you*, from my timeline. You — he — said again that he didn't cheat, and I wanted to believe him. I wanted it so much, but I couldn't. There's proof."

Mike wanted to defend the version of him in her head. "I can't believe I'd ever cheat on you, if we ended up together. I haven't slept with another woman since I met you."

"That's what he said." Her smile wasn't convincing.

"Maybe he's telling the truth?"

"You almost sound like you believe me."

He tilted her chin up with his finger, so he could hold her gaze as he spoke. "I'm in love with you. I want to believe that we'll spend the rest of our lives together. Help me?" Hearing her theory would give him ammo to refute it.

Because all mental issues were so easily dealt with. *God.* He was grasping at straws.

She studied his face and then said, "All right. But I'm warning you, when you hear everything, you'll want to have me committed."

It was a risk he'd have to take.

"I think my cousin had something to do with it. She dabbles in magic—"

"In... 2030?"

"2031. And I still can't wrap my mind around that. Anyway, she gave me a statue of an old god—a good-luck charm of sorts—when you and I got married. I think it's somehow making me dream of what our relationship could have been like."

"So we weren't like this?" Despite himself, he was fascinated by her story.

"No. For one, I didn't know we'd end in heartache."

He cupped her cheek, and she smiled. "I'm okay," she said. "You're not the one who did it, yet. To answer your question, this—with you—is close to my memories but different. When we were together, I centered my life on you. Stopped singing. Stayed home, waiting for the phone to ring."

"That's why you won't give me your number?"

She glared. "I won't give you my number because the *me* who'll answer if you call has no clue who you are. You said you ran into her on the street."

This was so confusing. How could she keep track of such an elaborate fantasy? "And in these dreams, you hold back from falling for me?"

"I try to."

"Yeah, I've got this irresistible boyish charm."

"Jerk." But she was smiling when she batted his shoulder.

"And how do you get here?"

She looked at him as if he'd asked the dumbest thing ever. "I go to sleep."

"So all the nights you didn't show...?"

"I didn't want to see you."

144

He gave a slow nod. "Which means you control it."

"Sort of. Only this morning I realized that whenever I saw you I'd wished for it in the vicinity of the statue."

"The one your cousin gave you at our wedding."

"Yes."

He stood and paced the length of the room. "This is nuts, Ana." It had consistency, and she had a response to his every question, but to believe it, he had to believe in magic, and magic didn't exist in 2031 *or* 2015.

"Okay. How's this? You and Derek grew up together. You briefly dated his sister, who's now your best friend—she hasn't called me since our divorce, by the way. When he first opened *Arbore's-San Francisco*, he took you on as a manager. His bitch of an ex fired you when she took over, and you're now helping him out as a chef because Nicholas was in a car crash with the boy toy he insists is nothing more than his sous chef, but we all know he's got the hots for."

Mike gaped. Crazy or not, she'd done her research. Still, it proved nothing. "All this says is that you've looked into my past."

Ana chewed on the inside of her cheek. "Okay. What's the date today?"

"October twenty-third, 2015."

"*Awesome.*" Her face lit up. "That's when Derek told you about the London restaurant. You came home from your shift, and we celebrated."

Mike sank in the armchair across from her, needing some distance to clear his head. "Derek told me not to go to work for a couple days. My behavior has been kind of erratic."

"Shit." She sighed. "I got nothing, then."

"You've got me." His gut knotted with the crushing certainty he wasn't enough to help her.

Chapter Sixteen

Mike's phone rang, and Bella jumped.

It was weird, what made the body react. She lay alongside the man who hurt her, in a makeshift nest of his covers that carried his scent, but his old ringtone sent her down a spiral of gloom. They used to love this song. Together.

Mike excused himself to the kitchen, to answer. At this hour, it was either work or a family emergency, and there had been none of the latter this year, so Bella relaxed. The kitchen was only separated from the living room by a counter, but she wouldn't have listened in anyway. She never checked texts or browsing history either. If she had, she might have caught on to him sooner.

She looked up as Mike returned.

Even slack jawed and wide eyed, he looked incredible from down here, his body long and lean and hard. His cock was half erect, and if Bella wasn't still sore from earlier, she'd have jumped him. "What happened?" she asked instead.

"It was Derek. He bought a restaurant in London. He wants me to spearhead it and offered me equal partnership."

Bella managed a smile she didn't feel. "I hate to say, I told you so. *Oh, wait. I don't.*"

"But how did you...?" He shook his head. "He hasn't even told Amanda yet. You couldn't have known."

"Unless I did." *Because the past didn't change.*

"Unless you did. Fuck. You're telling the truth. You're from the future." He spoke slowly, as if tasting the flavor of each word before he voiced it.

She nodded.

He dug his fingers in his hair and tugged. "So we've really been together for years? We were married?"

"Yes and yes."

"Are my parents — "

"Alive and annoying you."

"And I cheated on you? I can't imagine doing that."

She winced. "Neither could I."

"Are you sure?"

Bella rolled her shoulders, to keep from rolling her eyes.

He sank down next to her, holding her gaze. "I'm so sorry."

"I know."

"Did we...? Were there kids?"

"No. It was never the right time, and after a while we realized we liked our life without them."

Mike draped an arm around her shoulders, and she snuggled close. "Good," he said. "I mean, good that I – that future-me – didn't hurt anyone else. We need to fix this."

"We can't. Nothing changes. I didn't give you my number, but we still saw each other again. Tonight you didn't go to work, you said you'd been a jerk – "

"I believe I said I was acting erratically."

" – and still Derek is sending you to London. It all leads to the same future. There's nothing we can do."

"Then why would this god guy send you back?"

She'd wondered too, and now she had her answer. Xochipilli sent her back, to help her make peace with what happened. She needed to accept her life for what it was and put the past behind. It was why she'd felt so drowsy after making her last wish. This was how she'd be happy.

She should feel exhilarated. No matter what she did differently, nothing would change. It meant their future wasn't her fault, despite her mistakes. Mike would always sleep with the redhead, because things happened, and Bella couldn't control them.

"He wanted me to accept that you and I are over, I guess," she said. Her throat felt raw, and her lungs were *constricted. How did her heart have room to beat, when this huge weight pressed down on her chest?*

"He didn't have to involve me, then. He could make you dream actual dreams."

She shrugged. "Who knows how Aztec gods work?"

Mike laid a kiss on her temple. "But you can stay. You have to. We'll find a way, and we'll start over. Do things right. I won't cheat if I know I'm going to lose you."

"If you cared about losing me, you wouldn't have cheated anyway."

So simple. Lesson learned. She should wake up now and break the meddling statue into a million pieces, to ensure she didn't return here.

But first... "Make love to me, Mike." One last time.

* * * *

Bella woke to the gray light filtering in through the tinted window panes of her living room. Had she slept through the day and to the next morning? She was in her armchair, still clutching her phone. The screen read 7:23 PM. Long nap. Visiting past-Mike in mid-day when it was night for him was a first; their timelines were parallel till now. Magic had its own rules, though.

Tears stung Bella's eyes, but she'd cried enough. For the first time since she discovered Mike's infidelity, she felt like talking about him, and there was only one person she could be completely honest with.

She called her cousin.

Half an hour later, Angie pulled over in front of Bella's building. She must have heard Bella's distress over the phone, because she didn't bother parking. Just stopped the car in the middle of the street.

Bella slid into the passenger seat. "I believe you," she said, as she shut the door. "About magic, about Xochipilli... about everything."

Angie shut off the engine and faced her. "Explain."

"First, I thought you might want this back. He's served his purpose." Bella handed her the figurine of Xochipilli.

Angie cupped it with both hands and frowned. "Still not following, I'm afraid."

"He's been sending me to the past."

Angie's look of incomprehension had a cartoonish quality. Her brows arched, and her eyes were as big as saucers. "You're shitting me."

"I wish." Bella slapped a hand over her mouth. "No, I don't."

Someone honked behind them, and Angie muttered something about turning him into a frog. She didn't pull out though, and the guy maneuvered around them, yelling and cursing.

"So. Past. Time travel. Tell me more," Angie said.

"It's been on and off for months now. Since the night before we signed the papers for the divorce. I go to sleep, and I dream of Mike, back when we started dating. At least, I thought they were just dreams. But they're not. It's really him."

"In the past."

"*Yes.*" Bella kept talking—about what she'd done wrong in her relationship with Mike; about her lingering feelings for him and how she blamed herself for his cheating; about the depression she'd hidden for this long. And about the statue.

Angie patted Bella's knee and gave her awkward, cramped hugs, but mostly she listened. And from her expression, she believed every word.

"But Xochipilli doesn't work this way," she said when Bella was done. "I asked him for help before, with Lexi, and he led her to her true love. He wouldn't put you through all that, to help you get over Mike. Maybe he meant for you to try again."

Bella shook her head. "If he wanted us to patch things up, wouldn't the *now* have changed? I mean, I told Mike what he did wrong. If he stayed faithful afterward, we wouldn't be here."

"I guess you're right." Angie frowned. "When you went back, you kept him from meeting his Ana. If that was your actual past, you wouldn't be divorced from him now, because you would never have met him."

"This is making my head hurt," Bella said. "I think I need a drink."

One drink turned to several, and by the time she got into bed, she was too exhausted to dream or make wishes.

"Goodnight, Xochipilli," she said to the statue on her nightstand. "You're a tenacious little fucker."

The statue smiled, and Bella drifted off.

Chapter Seventeen

Ana wasn't coming back.

Mike had felt her decision in her body, tense even as it yielded beneath him.

He'd seen it in her eyes, red with unshed tears.

She'd carved it on his back, with her nails.

Ana had said *goodbye* and left him behind, broken and alone.

He hadn't said his last word, though. It took him minutes to find the single recording studio near *Arbore's*, and this was the third morning in a row he waited for her.

This time he knew she wouldn't recognize him. Worse, she might remember him as the spooky stranger who accosted her one time, insisting they were sleeping together. He was prepared for that.

Ana might have given up on them, but he hadn't. Wouldn't.

Today was the first day of the rest of their lives.

His confidence wavered when she rounded the corner. She wore dark, oversized sunglasses, and her pale-blond hair was gathered atop her head in a messy bun. She looked dazzling in the morning light, and Mike realized he'd never seen her in direct sunlight before. Even that day he ran into her while looking for *his* Ana, the sky had been overcast.

He'd never before seen her this glowing or this upbeat. There was a bounce in her step, as she approached the entrance of the building he'd been watching for the last couple hours. This Ana was sixteen years lighter, but most of all, she was unburdened by the knowledge the man she loved had been a cheater.

How could he ever cheat on her? He still couldn't wrap his mind around it. Hell, he'd gone monogamous for her. He believed in time travel for her. But she said the future couldn't change, and if she was right—no matter what—he'd be an asshole, and he'd slip, and he'd break her heart. Could he approach her, knowing that? She seemed so happy and carefree. She might hold on to this, if she never met him.

His heart would wither and die, and he'd spend his life settling for less, but Ana would be happy.

Would she?

What he saw now was a moment in her life. Could he tell with absolute certainty that her next sixteen years would be better without him than with him? No. And at the end of the day, he refused to accept that he was unable to control his dick and would blow up his relationship with Ana for a mere fuck.

He'd talk to her.

Though it'd have to wait till she came back out, since in the time it took him to decide, she'd disappeared inside the building.

What followed were the longest four hours of his life.

A headache was building at the base of his skull when she reemerged. Mike watched her hug a stylish brunette in her thirties. As she pulled back from the hug, the woman looked right at him, and then said something to Ana. Mike didn't catch what it was, but Ana spun his way with a frown. He chanced a wave, and she narrowed her eyes and strode across the road to him. The older woman studied them, her arms crossed and her mouth drawn in a thin line.

"You again." Ana stopped a couple feet from him. She didn't seem happy to see him.

Mike ached to hold her close, but she wasn't *his* Ana yet. He decided to focus on her words instead of the daggers her eyes threw. "You remember me."

"I remember saying I'd call the police next time you showed up." She pointed over her shoulder with her thumb. "Cassandra is ready to dial."

"I'm not here to cause trouble," Mike said. "I know I freaked you out last time, but now I have answers."

"Cassandra says you've been staring at the studio for three days."

Had she even heard him? "Ana, there is something I need to tell you, and it'll be hard for you to believe, but I swear it's the truth."

"You keep saying my name like you know me."

So they were doing this here. Okay by him. "I do know you. I'm supposed to know you. We're meant to be together. Just let me explain, please." And... he sounded crazy.

"I think I've heard enough." She took a step back. She was leaving.

Mike couldn't let her go. He clasped her wrist, lightly, praying she wouldn't feel threatened and run. "Please give me five minutes," he said. It wouldn't be enough, but he had to try.

Her eyes were narrowed to slits, and her voice rose above conversational levels. "You stalk me. Show up at my recording studio. Spout your garden-variety-stalker spiel about how we're *meant to be*. Why would I ever listen to you?"

He was prepared for this question. "Because if you get to know me, I'll remind you of that cat you had. The one that hated everyone but you, because with you, he was home."

She schooled her features to remain impassive, but not before he saw the shock in her eyes. "How do you know about my cat?"

"You told me."

She snorted. "When?"

"Two nights ago."

"Let me guess. We had sex again, and I again don't remember it."

"We didn't. It wasn't you. It was future-you." This wasn't going well. "I know it sounds impossible, but a woman looking exactly like you walked into the restaurant I work at, a few weeks ago. We left together. I can prove it. People saw us. They saw her again the next night. She kept coming back, and then she stopped. First time I met you, I thought you were her."

"And she just happened to also have my name?" She wrapped her denim jacket tighter around her. She was still ready to flee, but she was listening.

"She did. She kept disappearing on me, and two nights ago she showed up with a story I couldn't believe. She said she was you, but from the future. That she was my wife. My ex-wife. That we got a divorce"—he'd leave out the reason, for now—"and she was heartbroken, and she was somehow sent back, to… I don't know. She said it was to get over me, but I doubt it. I think it was so we could make things right."

She put more distance between them. "You *are* crazy. I have to go."

"Ana, please." Please, what? "Just come by *Arbore's* tonight. My entire brigade has seen us kiss. They've been making fun of me for acting like a lovesick kid. When you—when *she* wouldn't show for days, I went nuts. I acted like a jerk. Because I'm in love with her. With you."

"You don't even know me."

"Come by *Arbore's*. Public place. Nothing to fear. I'm not working tonight, but I'll be there. I'll tell you every detail she's given me." An idea hit him, reviving his dying hope. "You have a cousin. Angie, right? She can do magic. Real magic. Call her. Ask her. She gave you a small statue of an Aztec god for our wedding. That's what's responsible for all this."

"I have to go."

"Call Angie. Give me a chance. Give us a chance."

She hurried to her friend without a look back.

She wasn't going to show tonight.

And yet, Mike would wait for her.

Forever.

Chapter Eighteen

Bella tossed a carton of juice in her cart. She was dying for some ice cream, but it wasn't good—for her throat or her figure. Damn. She stood in front of the freezer and studied the offerings anyway. So many flavors, and all tempting her to break the rules. In all honesty, she deserved a little treat. She hadn't wished for Mike all day. She'd thought about it, but didn't go through with it.

She had her eye on caramel swirl, when she caught Cassandra's reflection in the glass. She stood at the other end of the isle, looking Bella's way. *Busted.* Not interested in a sermon about the evil of unsaturated fats, Bella slid to the next freezer and pretended to ponder seafood, before turning to wave at her manager.

She'd been wrong. Cassandra wasn't looking at her, but glaring at a man to Bella's right. A man Bella had seen before.

The gorgeous stranger she'd met at the bar, weeks ago. His cornflower-blue eyes were impossible to forget.

What were the odds Cassandra knew him?

Bella didn't know why, but she didn't want Cassandra to see her watching. She ducked behind her cart, as Cassandra strode past and to the man. The same impulse made her leave her shopping behind and follow the two when Cassandra pulled the man around the corner. Bella was hidden from their view by shelves of cereal, but she could see their faces.

"No need to get violent," the man said. "You know I'd follow you anywhere." His grin was the opposite of Cassandra's frown.

"Why are you here?" Cassandra asked. "You lost. They're not getting back together, despite your best efforts. Fate has lost, and you finally have to leave me alone."

"You know they're both in pain when they're apart." He reached for her cheek, but Cassandra slapped his hand away.

"Ana is fine," she said. "She's getting her future back, and soon she'll find someone else."

Bella tried to make sense of what she heard. Cassandra had a hand in her breakup with Mike? This was impossible. She and Cassandra hadn't seen each other in years. Bella was the one who approached Cassandra, not the other way around.

"But she's not happy." The man turned to look straight at Bella. "Are you?"

Cassandra twirled her way too, and her face... rippled. For a split second, it morphed into a much younger visage. One Bella couldn't forget since seeing it on her phone. It was the woman Mike had cheated with.

Bella felt her jaw drop. "What the hell is going on? Cassandra?" She looked around, to see if anyone else had noticed, but nobody even glanced their way.

"Don't worry. They no longer... perceive us. We can have this little chat undisturbed." Still smiling, the man grabbed Cassandra's wrist. "I always find it funny that you keep your name when dealing with mortals," he said. "Now tell Anabella what a bad girl you've been."

"Let me go," Cassandra said, but his hold was so tight, his knuckles turned white.

"Tell her, or I will," he said.

Cassandra shut her mouth, her gaze defiant and stubborn. She looked young again, but no longer like Mike's lover — thank God.

"Okay," the man said. "First, let me introduce myself. I've had many names through the years, but you know me as Xochipilli."

This wasn't happening. Bella was asleep again.

"You're not dreaming, Anabella. Cassandra is the woman I told you about. The one who won't take me back, even though I love her more than life."

Cassandra made a disgusted sound in her throat and rolled her eyes.

"It's true, you stubborn woman." He turned back to Bella. "She and I made a pact recently, after playing Tug of War for thousands of years."

"Thousands of years. Because you're an ancient god, and she is…?"

"My destiny," he said.

Not very specific, but seeing he wouldn't elaborate, Bella asked, "What was the pact?"

"Tired of dancing around each other —"

"There was no dancing. You were harassing me."

Xochipilli ignored Cassandra's protest and continued. "We decided to choose a couple fated to be together, and see how they dealt with hardship and temptation. If they defied destiny and were better off apart, I'd stop pursuing her. If she lost, she'd give me another chance."

So, if Bella was to believe him... "You played with us?"

"That wasn't our agreement." Xochipilli gave Cassandra a stern look. "We were supposed to put temptation in your path and observe, not interfere further. When she took it upon herself to make you think Mike cheated, I did my best to get you to remember your love and how he couldn't have betrayed you."

There were two apparently immortal beings standing before her, and the only thing Bella could think to ask was, "Mike didn't cheat?"

"Cassandra, tell the young lady. Now, please."

Still not looking at her, Cassandra said, "I flirted with him in London. Tried to get him to come home with me, but he wouldn't. He never touched me. The pictures were fabricated."

"But I had them analyzed."

"Technology recognizes technology," Xochipilli said, "and Angela had no reason to look for magic."

Angela?

Angie.

"Why would you do this?" Bella asked Cassandra. She hated the tremble in her voice, but it wasn't weakness. It was suppressed anger. She wanted to choke the bitch.

"I thought you'd be better off without him," Cassandra whispered.

"No, you didn't. You only cared about winning your stupid bet."

"She's done worse, to prove a point," Xochipilli said. "She turned a poor man into a dog for six months."

Cassandra rolled her eyes. "It wasn't to prove a point. I loved him."

Bella had enough. "You two deserve each other," she said. "You may have lived thousands of years, but you have no clue what love is."

Xochipilli's smile vanished. "I swear I tried to help you."

"You wouldn't have had to, if you hadn't forced my arm," Cassandra told him.

"Instead of sending me to the past, you could have told me he never cheated," Bella said.

"And forfeited the bet," Cassandra said.

"You did that when you sent those pictures," he replied.

Cassandra shook her head. "You should have said so then, instead of going along with it. Doesn't count now."

"I wanted you to see fate always wins, no matter how you try to avoid it. And your fate is to be with me." Xochipilli let go of Cassandra's hand and brushed his fingertips over her cheek.

Cassandra glared but didn't pull away from his touch. "So you keep saying, but I can't see it."

He smiled again. "Just one date. Let me win you back."

Bella threw her arms in the air. "Shut up, both of you. God, you guys are terrible."

Xochipilli tried to say something. "I said, *shut up*," Bella yelled. She was being disrespectful to a deity with the ability to send her to the past. He could probably obliterate her, but she was done with him and his psycho-ex. "I've heard enough. I have to talk to Mike."

She left them to their bickering and hurried out of the supermarket, dialing Mike's number from memory. Deleting him from her contacts had served no real purpose, but she'd done it in her effort to erase him from her life.

Her call went to voicemail, and she growled. She needed to get a hold of him.

Doubt inched its way into her thoughts. She'd turned him down repeatedly and refused to listen to his claims of innocence. What would she say now? Would the truth do, wacky as it was? She hadn't believed him. Why would he believe her?

It didn't matter. She'd try. He had, when the odds were against him.

She dialed again. Same result.

She swallowed her ego and called Tanya, who remained one of Mike's best friends and was more likely to talk to Bella than Derek was.

"Bella," Tanya said. "This is a surprise."

"I know. I'm sorry to bother you."

"No bother. I've been meaning to call you, but I wasn't sure you'd want to hear from me."

Bella shook her head, though she wasn't on video call and Tanya couldn't see her. "It's okay. It's all okay. I just need to find Mike. I've made a terrible mistake." She stopped herself before saying more. Mike was the one she owned an explanation to.

"He's in London."

It wasn't his usual visit, unless he'd changed his schedule. "Isn't it too early in the month?"

Tanya was quiet long enough for Bella to get antsy. Then she said, "I thought you knew. He's moving there."

Shit. Shit, shit, shit. *Fuck.* And Bella didn't have his European cell number, because how many digits could she have memorized? "Can you text me his contact info there, please? It's urgent."

After kicking him out of their place and selling it, Bella now wanted him to scrap his plans about moving to England and start over with her. When they were officially divorced.

Worst timing ever.

Tanya forwarded her his electronic data, but Mike didn't answer any of the eighteen times she tried him. It occurred to Bella that it was three in the morning for him, and he was probably asleep, but she kept trying until she got home, despite her car's electronic voice insisting she not talk and drive.

She got to her loft and headed straight for Xochipilli's statue, or where it had last been. It wasn't there.

Or anywhere.

She called Mike again. And again. And several times in a row, but he was unreachable.

When her eyelids grew heavy, she wished she could visit past-Mike. Perhaps Xochipilli was still listening.

Chapter Nineteen

Mike was about to give up and go home. He'd had enough teasing for the night, and Ana obviously wasn't going to show.

The kitchen closed a few minutes ago, so his plans for a romantic dinner were spoiled. They were too farfetched anyway. Why would she have dinner with a stranger? And a crazy one at that?

Not that he wouldn't come back tomorrow. And the day after that. And when he started his shifts again until he left for London, he'd glance at the door every so often. Because he knew she'd come. She had to. They were meant to be. They'd fallen in love before, overcoming time itself.

Ana would come.

Just not tonight.

He called Mario over and asked for a third Espresso. "For the road."

Pity swam in Mario's eyes. "You got it, man." He returned soon, holding another steaming, tiny cup.

Espresso was supposed to be gulped down, but Mike took his time with it. As much as his mind told him tonight wasn't his night, his body refused to carry him away from the chance to see Ana.

His body knew best. It tensed at the gust of air whooshing in, before Ana stepped in, her long hair flying around her face. She held her skirt down with one hand, fighting the wind that seemed to want to undress her.

Or take her to Mike as soon as possible.

The door thumped her forward and slid shut, and the wind died together with all sound from the kitchen. The brigade fell silent, everyone's attention on Ana.

"Get back to work." Derek slapped the pass. "Kitchen won't clean itself." He approached Ana, who stood still, and asked, "Have you eaten? Can I get you something?"

She stared at Mike as she shook her head. "No, thanks. I'm fine. But— This is going to sound weird, but have you seen me before? In here?" she asked Derek.

Mike hadn't explained the insanity that was his relationship with Ana, other than mentioning they had some issues.

Derek gave Ana a strange look. "I've seen you twice, if I remember correctly."

"And I was talking to him?" Ana indicated Mike with a tilt of her head.

Mario chuckled. "I don't think what you were doing was talking."

Grant snapped his towel across the server's head. "Idiot."

"You only exchanged a few words," Derek said. "And then there was the kiss Mario is being a dick about."

Mike realized he hadn't moved since he saw her. He should stand. Motion for her to come closer. Do a tap dance. Anything but sit there, praying she didn't run again.

"A kiss." She chewed on her bottom lip. "I changed my mind. Do you serve alcohol?"

Derek smiled. "We have wine."

"Bring us a bottle of white? I think this is going to be a long night." She frowned. "Or are you closing?"

The few patrons still left would be gone soon, but Derek said, "Mike can lock up when you're done. Don't worry about it."

Mike got enough command over his legs, to stand when she reached his table. She sat before he could pull out her chair, but it was okay. She was there, and if things went his way, he'd get several more chances to be gallant.

He returned to his seat and took her in. Her eyes seemed younger than *his* Ana's, but other than that, they were the same person. He longed to take her hand. To feel her skin against his. Judging from her squared shoulders and how she fidgeted with her phone, she'd bolt if he made a sudden movement.

It took effort for him to maintain an impassive expression. "I'm glad you came."

"Incredibly, Angie admitted to being a witch. *God.* Listen to me. As if I accused her of stealing my favorite jeans. She said she casts spells, and she knew that Xochiguy when I said he was an Aztec god with a weird name."

"So you believe me?"

She made an incredulous sound. "I wouldn't go that far."

Derek showed up with the wine and poured them each a glass.

Ana polished hers off and refilled it. "Let's just say I'm willing to hear you out. But people know where I am and will come after you if I disappear, so don't do anything stupid."

"I wouldn't."

"Talk, then."

Where to begin?

He took it from the top and described the first time future-Ana showed up at *Arbore's*. "I couldn't take my eyes off her."

This Ana blushed.

"Come on," Mike said. "You know you're gorgeous. I couldn't believe my luck when she said she'd wait for my shift to end."

He glossed over the specifics of what followed, but wasn't shy about sharing the thoughts he'd had the next day and how he jumped every time the restaurant's door opened. "I hoped she'd come back. And she did." For more sex. This Ana would think he was a sex-a-holic.

The more they talked, the more he saw she was the woman he loved, only less jaded. He'd see to it that she remained this way.

"How many times did you see her?" she asked.

"Enough to know she was the one for me. I was a dog until the night I met her, but she made me lose interest in all other women."

"And you say she came from the future. Our future."

"I know it's hard to accept, but she knew things. She told me Derek would call and ask me to go to London, and he did. Offered me half a restaurant there, *as she said he would*."

Ana took a swig of her wine. "Angie says that's possible, in theory. That magic, or her god, can do that. But I still don't get why. Why not go to her timeline's Mike and patch things up?"

And this was the hard part. He'd debated whether he should reveal this, but he didn't want to lie, even by omission. "He cheated. I did. In the future." Ana sat back, a frown on her face, and Mike rushed to elaborate. "She said someone emailed her pictures of me with another woman, but I can't believe I'd ever do that to her. To you."

She met his gaze, her face a mask carved in stone. "So what do you want now, Mike?"

You. Everything. You. "What do you mean?" he asked, playing for time. He needed to tone it down, or he'd lose her for good.

"I mean, you and I are supposed to be soul mates, according to this farfetched story of yours. But I don't know you. You're cute, and you don't give off a creepy vibe — which, *yay* — but this can only get you so far. I'm not going to fall head over heels with you, so we can pick things up where you and this other Ana left off. And where do I fit into your plans for London? I'm working on my career here; I can't drop it all for a stranger and the promise of a fairytale that has already ended up with you cheating on me. So I'm asking again — what do you want?"

Her reasoning was infallible, damn it. Still — no risk, no gain. "I want one date," Mike said. "We've done things the other way around, with the crazy sex and the forbidden passion that transcends logic. Now I want to give this a proper try. Give me one date. One chance to woo you. I'll cook, or we can go dancing. A movie. Anything you want. If we click, we take it from there and see where it leads us. Long-distance relationships can work. They do sometimes. I mean, if we really like each other." He realized he was rambling, and shut his mouth.

Ana fiddled with the white linen tablecloth, avoiding his gaze until his heart sunk in his stomach. He was about to concede defeat, when she looked up and straight at him. "One date. Public place. No pressure, and no further negotiations if things don't work out the way you want."

His smile threatened to split his face in two. "Deal."

Epilogue

A hard-rock band was rehearsing inside Bella's head. A bad, out-of-tune hard-rock band.

She didn't drink last night, but this felt like the world's worst hangover.

She sat up and lowered her feet to the hardwood floor. *Hardwood?* Her new place was lined with marble.

She took in her surroundings and gasped. She wasn't at her loft, but in the apartment she'd shared with Mike.

Was she still dreaming?

Had Xochipilli come through, after all?

The pain in her head intensified, until her ears buzzed. Mental images swirled in her mind. *Mike.* Their first date at what became their favorite Chinese place, and the chaste peck on the lips that sealed the deal for her. She knew that night that she'd see him again.

But it hadn't been like that. Her first night with Mike had involved nothing chaste. It was all about lust and passion.

Whatever was happening to her demanded coffee.

Did the place still come with a *HouseSsistant5000*? She dragged her feet to the kitchen and clapped her hands. Might as well take advantage of the thing, if it was installed. "Start coffee," she said. The quiet whirring of the coffee machine made her smile, and she grabbed a mug in the two seconds the thing needed for its best aromatic brew.

A fresh onslaught of images filled her head and made her stumble. She gripped the edge of the stainless-steel sink, to steady herself, as new memories of the past sixteen years drew parallels to her existing ones.

She went to London with Mike *and* stayed in San Francisco with the promise to wait for him.

She waited tables at their bistro in England *and* pursued a career as a solo singer in the States, with the help of a manager who wasn't Cassandra.

But most importantly, she was divorced from Mike *and*—

Strong arms wrapped around her waist, making her jump. "Gotcha." Mike's throaty laugh by her ear gave her goosebumps, as he held her tighter, the hard planes of his chest and abs pressing against her back.

She squeezed her eyes shut and tried to wake up. If this was Xochipilli's idea of a joke, he was heartless and Cassandra was better off without him.

"Baby? Are you okay?" Mike kissed her neck and turned her to face him. "You're pale as a sheet."

She opened her eyes and looked up at him. When she was barefoot, he was six inches taller than her five-seven. His eyes were filled with concern but free of the pain that marred them last time they were this close.

Because here, now, she and Mike were still married.

They'd met sixteen years ago, when he came to her with an impossible story. And she believed him. He'd convinced her to go on a date with him, and chipped at her defenses until she couldn't resist their attraction. They'd weathered a long-distance relationship — many times over — when he was away for business or she was on tour.

She had a new record coming out this week.

And they were happy.

Was this her new reality, or was it another cruel game? "I didn't know you were back," she said after an eternity.

Mike arched an eyebrow, and she couldn't stop herself from smoothing it down with her fingers. "As if I'd miss our anniversary breakfast," he said.

Sixteen years together. They celebrated a different date than before.

Mike slanted his mouth over hers, and she poured all her love and the anguish that marked her last few months into the kiss.

When they broke apart, he lowered his hands to her hips and lead her backward to the table. "Sit and let me wow you with my world-famous pancakes."

She dropped to the nearest chair and watched from the side, as his back rippled and his arms flexed beneath his skin-tight T-shirt. He looked as good as ever, and she wanted to skip food in favor of more pleasurable things. Maybe she should. She didn't know if she had two hours or a day in this version of reality, and she'd hate to waste any of it.

But she'd missed this domesticity as much as anything. Being with past-Mike had been amazing, but she hadn't shared a life with him. This was her man. Her destiny.

And he wasn't hers anymore. Not really.

Bella wanted to weep.

"I almost forgot." Mike grinned at her and fished a white envelope out of his jeans' back pocket. "You have fan-mail. The proper, pen-on-paper kind. Hope the sender is not a stalker." He held it out, waited for Bella to snatch it, and then flipped two pancakes into a large plate.

That was weird. Fan-mail went to the studio—weirder still that she knew that, because last she checked, her career had ended before it began. Her home address was printed on the back of the envelope, but the sender had identified themselves only by *A Fan*.

She ripped it open, retrieved the single piece of paper it held inside, and unfolded it with trembling hands.

> *I am infinitely sorry for the pain I have caused you and your Michael. It was all in the name of love, although I am ashamed to admit my years may have jaded my perspective. Please accept my apologies in the form of the life you were always meant to have.*
>
> *~X*

She read the words two more times, before their meaning sank in. This was her *happily ever after*.

"Is it terrible?" Mike placed a stack of pancakes in front of her. They were drizzled in maple syrup and topped with a dollop of butter. Three sizable slices of bacon completed the mouthwatering dish.

This was her new reality. Her only reality, now on. "Huh?" she asked.

"The letter. Is it terrible?"

"No." She tangled her fingers through his and returned his smile. She had her home, her man, and a breakfast that defied her perma-diet. "Everything is perfect."

Finally.

The End

If you want to see more of Xochipilli's meddling, don't miss *Magic at Work*.

For another glimpse at Cassandra, read *Furry Christmas*.

For Derek and Amanda's love story, check out *The Tenant*.

Keep up to date with all the latest news and information from Sotia Lazu at http://www.SotiaLazu.com

Acknowledgments

Thank you, Erin Dameron-Hill, for creating this gorgeous cover. I saw it and had to write a story for it.

Thank you, Jade Mulrooney, for coming up with the title and Anabella's name. They both worked perfectly!

Thank you Allyson Lindt for not letting me quit this any of the five million times I was about to, for your brilliant notes, and for your wonderful words of encouragement.

And as always, thank you, Andrei, for loving me, putting up with me, and not complaining when a manuscript emergency overtakes *another* romantic evening.

About the Author

Sotia loves romances with a twist and urban fantasy novels, always with vivid erotic elements. Her favorite characters to write are not conventional hero-material at first glance, and she enjoys making them fight for their happiness.

She shares her life and living quarters with her husband, their son, and two rescue dogs, one of which may be part-pony. Sappy movies make her bawl like a baby, and she wishes she could take in all the stray dogs in the world.

Also, she hates mornings!

www.ingramcontent.com/pod-product-compliance
Lightning Source LLC
Chambersburg PA
CBHW071234130626
46556CB00003B/998